Ringing in Love

PEGGY BIRD

author of *Sparked by Love* and *Unmasking Love*

CRIMSON ROMANCE

F+W Media, Inc.

Published by
Crimson Romance
an imprint of F+W Media, Inc.
10151 Carver Road, Suite 200
Blue Ash, OH 45242. U.S.A.
www.crimsonromance.com

ISBN 10: 1-4405-7042-6
ISBN 13: 978-1-4405-7042-1
eISBN 10: 1-4405-7043-4
eISBN 13: 978-1-4405-7043-8

Acknowledgments

When I started this journey as an author I had no idea that one of the benefits would be meeting so many remarkable women along the way. It's about time I thanked them. First, Jennifer, Julie, Jess, and Tara, the editors (past and present) at Crimson Romance who made my dreams come true and my books make sense. Next, my Crimson Romance Sisters. Thank you for friending, liking, sharing, tweeting, posting, voting, reading, and reviewing whenever I've asked. You are the most awesome support group anyone could have. Last, the amazing Lisa at Tasty Book Tours and Amy at Unwrapping Romance. (Dominic is for you, Amy.) Thank you all for your support and encouragement!

Chapter 1

"Damn it, Melody," Catherine Bennett said as she slammed into the dolly loaded with banker's boxes her assistant was supposed to be pulling. "You can't stop like that. This thing has no brake lights to warn me." As she steadied the pile of teetering boxes, she followed Melody's gaze to see what had distracted her. She should have known. A man. Dominic Russo, to be precise. And he was definitely a distraction. Mister Dark and Dangerous. Man candy. A professional bachelor with a reputation for notching his bedpost with a new name every few weeks. Name a cliché describing a sexy male, and he fit it. Hell, he owned it.

He also owned one of the most successful public relations firms in Philadelphia and was Catherine's biggest competitor.

"Damn is right," Melody said. "Hot damn."

Catherine bent and rubbed the shin that had borne the brunt of the collision. "You might want to add an 'ouch' in there."

Melody whipped around as quickly as she'd stopped. "Oops. Sorry, Catherine. Are you okay? Didn't mean to hurt you. I was just admiring the scenery." She returned her attention to the man who was now almost at the elevator bank. "Look at those shoulders! And the way he moves. I bet he's a great dancer—and you know what *that* means. He is definitely sex on legs. Wonder who he is?"

"Your encyclopedic knowledge of Philadelphia gossip is failing you. The 'scenery,' as you put it, is Dominic Russo. The Russo Group has offices on the fifteenth floor."

"Of course! Shoulda looked at his face instead of his ass." Melody started toward the elevator again. "If you'd told me my days in our new office building would be brightened by sightings of the sexiest man in the city, I'd have been happier about moving here."

"I'd have used it, believe me, if I'd known it would have stopped you from complaining about all the work it took to move the office."

"You know how much I hate change and loved the old building." Melody looked across the lobby again. "Although the old building never offered us something like that to look at. On the other hand, now that we're in the same building as our competition, we'll always have to be careful what we say when we're …"

The service elevator door began to close, and Catherine interrupted Melody's latest reservations about the new office arrangements to yell, "Hold the elevator!" to her staffer Tom.

But before Tom could hit the "door open" button, Dominic Russo made a graceful move to his left and grabbed the door.

"Thanks," Catherine said as she and Melody pushed the dolly into the elevator.

"Happy to help. Moving's hard enough without having to wait endlessly for elevators." He smiled and the temperature in the lobby spiked. "You're Catherine Bennett, aren't you? I'm Dominic Russo."

"Of course. We've actually met …"

He nodded. "After you spoke at the business roundtable about your firm's approach to socially responsible marketing and business practices. You had so many people trying to talk to you that day, I didn't know if you'd remember me. I enjoyed your presentation. When you get settled, maybe you'd consider repeating it to my staff. I don't imagine I did it justice when I tried to relay the information."

Not remember meeting him? Was he kidding? He was impossible to forget.

If the rumors were to be believed, most of the women in the city would agree. Interesting, because he wasn't handsome in a classic, young god kind of way. His jawline was a bit too strong and his nose a bit too aquiline for the perfect image of the divine.

The bits of silver beginning to show in his thick, dark hair and the lines around his eyes and mouth put him out of the age range of most Hollywood hotties.

But all that was unimportant compared to the devastating smile currently aimed at Catherine and the deep, dark, espresso brown eyes that seemed to say he knew everything worth knowing about a woman merely by looking at her. Any woman he turned that look on would have her knees melted in two seconds flat with the rest of her quickly following.

And then there was the body Melody had drooled over. Not to mention the wrapping it came in. Even in Philly's humid summer heat Mister Sex on Legs looked cool and unruffled. The dark suit he wore fit as if he had grown it like skin, not had it tailored. The accompanying white shirt was crisp and unwrinkled, the dark gold and black paisley print tie in a perfect knot, the matching pocket square precisely placed.

Catherine, on the other hand, was both ruffled and wrinkled. Her long hair was mostly pulled back into a messy ponytail; her jeans and T-shirt were rumpled and dusty. There were, she was sure, tracks of perspiration running down her neck and arms from helping to load the dolly with the boxes of client records she didn't trust to the movers. To top it off, she must reek; she hadn't showered yet today.

Naturally, Dominic Russo not only looked good, he smelled good. Like a gingerbread man.

Right. The hot guy smells like Christmas cookies. Nice, Catherine. Not some sensuous fragrance. A kid's holiday treat. You're really out of practice, aren't you?

She would prefer to think she was relying on food imagery because she'd skipped breakfast, but in truth she *was* out of practice. Unless he was a client, staff member, or sub-consultant, she hadn't thought about, dated, or otherwise paid attention to any man, sexy or otherwise, for a long time. With a business to grow and a teenaged son to raise, she didn't have time for a social life. At least, that's what she told her family and friends. What she admitted only to herself was she hadn't recovered from having her ex-husband leave her for another woman. She wasn't about to take the chance of having her ego battered again by a man who would use her for what he wanted then move on to the next female who crossed his path.

Although even at her best, she would have known better than to waste her time thinking about Dominic Russo in any capacity except as someone who did the same thing she did for a living. He was like the statues of perfectly formed men in the art museum. She might like looking at them, but they were blind to women like her, used to lots of attention, and off limits to the masses. He wasn't for amateurs.

Come to think of it, though, he *was* paying attention to her at the moment, waiting for a response to his request. Which was what she should be thinking about instead of mentally concocting some weird thought mixture of art museums, marble statues, and Christmas cookies. If she didn't say something soon, he was going to think she was an idiot.

Finally she got out, "I'd be happy to talk to your staff. But you're right; it'll have to be after we get ourselves settled."

"Not to worry. We'll be here when you're ready." As he let go of the door, he flashed another of his heat-inducing smiles, which Catherine was sure could not only melt knees but also the hooks on a bra. Lord, even her perfectly straight copywriter Tom was blushing from its high wattage. And Melody was speechless, for the first time in all the years Catherine had known her.

Oh, for heaven's sake, she wanted to say to her staff as the elevator began to rise to the tenth floor. *We don't have time for this. We have an office to get set up and clients to attend to.*

* * *

Dominic hadn't been in his office more than fifteen minutes when Edie Martin, his creative director, stormed in.

"What were you thinking, Dominic, letting The Bennett Group lease space in our building? Do you really think it's wise to have that group of newbie pretenders eavesdropping in the elevator every day when they're the biggest threat to our business?"

"It's Bennett and Associates, Edie. If you're going to complain about them, at least get the name right. And I'd hardly call them 'newbie pretenders.' They're one of the up and coming PR firms in the city. Everyone in the industry is talking about their approach as cutting edge."

"Why are you letting them in our building where they can spy on us and steal our clients?"

"It's not 'our' building. It's my building." He took the papers she'd been waving around as she spoke. "Catherine Bennett's firm has all the qualifications to be a good tenant, and I've had a hard time filling the space the engineering firm left when it moved. Besides, we already have several other threats to our business, as you describe them, in the building and we've been fine."

"But the other communications firms aren't—*she's* the one— *they're* the people who've been getting too much of the work we should have gotten."

"We have more than enough clients to keep us busy. And we're on track to have the most profitable year in a decade. I'm not worried Bennett and Associates will listen in on our plans through the HVAC system and we'll go under." He could see she was not responding to his attempts to make light of her concerns. "Why don't you think of it another way—now we have all our strongest competitors in one place so *we* can watch *them*."

Edie's face brightened a bit. "Oh, I never thought of it that way. Maybe you're right. Maybe it's a brilliant plan. I hope so, Dominic."

"Now, other than to bitch about Catherine Bennett what brought you to my office this lovely Monday?"

When Edie left, the thought of Catherine Bennett didn't go with her. Dominic's morning encounter with Ms. Bennett had been a welcome start to the day. In spite of being a bit sweaty and in clothes miles away from the stylish suit she'd worn the first time he'd met her, she was stunning. Her olive skin and her dark chocolate brown hair and eyes, which didn't fit with her WASP-y name, had intrigued him from the first. Still did, even though now he knew from a little background research that her coloring was from an Italian heritage as deep as his own. And there wasn't a man alive—well, a straight one—who wouldn't fantasize about the luscious curves even moving-day clothes couldn't hide. She wasn't some stick-thin model who served as a hanger for the latest designer's ideas of fashion. She had the body of a real woman. A real woman with considerable ability and the drive to take her firm all the way to success. It was quite a combination.

Dominic had wanted to get to know Catherine Bennett ever since he'd seen her give her presentation. Mostly he'd wanted to see if she was as smart and interesting one-on-one as she'd sounded on the dais. And he wouldn't mind finding out if she was as sexy in a more intimate situation as she was when she walked across a room in her pencil skirt and stilettos. He was bored to tears with the business dates he'd been stuck with for what seemed like an eternity. Catherine Bennett looked, sounded, and acted different.

And it wouldn't hurt to size up the woman who was making such a splash in his industry. Mixing business and pleasure was what he did on a regular basis. Most of his recent social life, including the women he escorted to the theater or dinner, had been more about marketing his business than about anything personal. At least if he were doing the mixing with Ms. Bennett, he might actually enjoy what he felt he had to do to keep his company on top.

A fixture in public relations and advertising in Philadelphia for more years than Dominic cared to think about, The Russo Group was the biggest, the most highly regarded, most sought after communications firm in the city. Catherine Bennett had only been on the scene for a half dozen or so years, but she'd made a name for herself in a niche he'd never thought about—marketing and advertising for socially responsible companies who wanted to do more than make a profit at any price. He admired someone who could find a new facet to a business he thought he knew cold and owned outright.

He'd told Edie the truth about how he viewed Bennett and Associates—there was plenty of business for both of them. But the fact was, relocating to the building where the big boys played meant Catherine Bennett was moving up in his world. It wouldn't hurt to keep an eye on her.

Or was he making business excuses to do what he wanted to do for personal reasons? And did it matter anyway?

• • •

"Ah … Catherine, someone's here to see you." Melody's voice sounded confused or nervous. Something. Certainly not like her usual self.

"I don't have anything on my calendar, do I? Who is it?"

"He's not on your calendar. And he's on his way back now." The call ended abruptly. Very unlike her usually efficient office administrator. And why was she working the phones anyway?

Catherine put down the phone and looked up as Mister Sex on Legs sauntered into her office. That explained it.

"Mister … ah … Dominic. What a nice surprise. What can I do for you?" Catherine tried to be more calm and collected than Melody had been. All she could really be was grateful she had an important client meeting later in the day and had worn her favorite cobalt blue suit, the one she knew was flattering to both her figure and her coloring. Because to hold her own in the same room with this visitor who always looked like he'd stepped out of *GQ* took the best she had.

Dominic Russo must have a closet the size of Rhode Island. In the two weeks she'd been in the building, she couldn't remember seeing him in the same suit twice. Not that she was keeping track. Okay, yes, she was keeping track. She didn't know why, but she was.

Today's suit was a navy pinstripe number with a white dress shirt and a light blue patterned tie that looked like a William Morris print. A white pocket square peeked out of the pocket over his well-toned pecs. The man knew how to dress. And call attention to his assets.

Oh, for God's sake. Pay attention to something other than his body, Bennett. What is wrong with you, anyway? You don't behave like this.

She forced herself to stop staring at his chest and glanced around the room, hoping her office made a good impression. It looked tidy, at least. Although her artwork hadn't been hung yet, all the furniture was in place: her glass-topped desk and small conference table, the cozy little couch covered in a bright red fabric, the Herman Miller Aeron chair for her, and a visitor's chair next to her desk.

"I wanted to make sure you'd gotten settled," Dominic said. "Although from looking around, I'd say you've done more in the past two weeks than many people manage to do in a month. Your artwork in the reception area is stunning, by the way, especially the image of the woman. I like it. Local artist?"

"Yes, a woman named Jamie Lutz. Thanks for noticing."

"I hope everything about the space was the way you wanted it to be when you moved in."

His interest puzzled her. "Does the building owner hire you to check on all the new tenants this way?"

"You didn't know I'm the building owner?"

She was sure her surprise was visible. "I thought the owner was DR Investments Limited."

He said nothing, seeming to wait for the penny to drop.

Which it did. "Oh, DR. Dominic Russo. Dear God, how could I have been so obtuse."

"You're anything but obtuse. I'm sure there are other tenants who don't know. The management company that handles all the transactions doesn't advertise it, and neither do I."

"But if I'd done my due diligence, I'd have found out. I didn't dig very deep, obviously. When the agent showed me the space and told me the price, I was so excited I didn't do much other than talk to some of your other tenants. All of them, by the way, raved about the building and the management, in case you wondered."

"Good to hear. And I'm happy you're settling in so well." He motioned to the chair next to her desk, which she took to be asking if he could sit.

"Please. Sit. I'm being rude." She returned to her desk chair. "It's been a pretty smooth transition. It's a great building. The location is perfect and the layout very creative. Did you have a hand in designing it?"

"Can't take credit for it, but it is what attracted me to the space. The original developer had gone bankrupt, and it was being sold at a good price when I was looking for new offices. My staff was working in such close quarters, I was beginning to think I'd have to insist they marry each other."

"We were almost there, too, although on a much smaller scale."

"You've come a long way in a short time, haven't you? I've admired your work and how fast you've become such an influence in the business." His killer smile was back, which almost distracted her enough that she missed the compliment he'd paid her.

"It feels like a long time and a short way, but thanks. I'm flattered."

"Not flattery. Just the truth." He rose from the chair and extended his hand. "I won't keep you any longer. I only wanted to make sure everything was as promised. I know you've met the building manager—if you have any problems at all, let him know."

When she took his hand, a pulse of electricity went up her arm, startling her enough she had to swallow a gasp. It warmed her all the way to the base of her neck and down her chest. He clasped her hand with both of his, his eyes holding hers in a look so warm she wanted to turn up the air conditioning. She also wanted to keep the conversation going so she didn't lose the connection with him.

"Uh … yes … the building manager." She swallowed hard. "He's been great. About getting movers in and out, I mean, stuff like that." *Stuff like that?* Where was her skill with words when she really needed it?

Dominic didn't say anything right away, seeming to be as reluctant as she was to break the contact between them. Finally he released her hand. "I'm glad he was helpful." He moved toward the door. "But let me know if you have a problem he can't solve. I'm sure I'll be seeing you around the building." And he was gone.

Catherine sank back into her chair feeling like all the life had left the room, along with most of the air in her lungs.

Chapter 2

Catherine certainly did see Dominic around the building, almost every day. If he wasn't at the coffee stand where she went first thing for her caffeine fix, he was strolling in the front door as she waited for the elevator. They rode together to their respective floors most mornings. She'd get off at the tenth floor with the faint smell of his body wash or aftershave or cologne or whatever it was in her nose. It was an extremely pleasant if sometimes distracting way to start the morning.

He always seemed happy to see her, chatting, making her laugh with some gossip from the building or their industry. Over the weeks, they exchanged bits of personal information. They had a mutual passion for the Sixers, a mistrust of the new coach of the Eagles, and an interest in art. She talked about her son. He passed on stories about local politicians, many of whom he'd done election campaign work for. It was amazing what one could learn in the time it took to walk across the lobby of a building, wait for an elevator, and travel ten floors. For all his reputation as a high-profile player, he never came on too strong, never pushed to make their conversation anything other than casual. Although he made a couple joking references to having lunch someday, he wasn't serious, she was sure.

She started to think of their morning chats as the beginning of a lobby-and-elevator relationship. She'd never had anything like it before. It was fun, but more importantly, it seemed simple and safe.

And if there was anything Catherine Alessandro Bennett needed at this point in her life, it was something that was both. Between her rapidly growing business and her equally fast growing teenaged son, she had enough complications and risk in her life. More, in fact, than at any other time in her thirty-eight years.

Though she'd been a stay-at-home mom after Noah was born, when he'd entered kindergarten she'd been eager to return to work at the PR firm where she'd been an account exec. Andy, her then-husband, had said he wanted her to continue focusing on their child. After a tough negotiation, he'd grudgingly given in to the idea of her taking on a few clients as a freelancer. Developing public relations and advertising campaigns for a client or two would not only help her keep up with the world she'd left when she'd become a mother, but also give her a creative outlet for her talents.

It was all that and more. The freelance jobs she picked up from her old company increased with every month. Then she started attracting clients on her own. She had to hire an assistant—which was how she met Melody Mason—to keep it all going. Then a second creative type. And another.

Her business model changed as she became interested in, and acquired a reputation for skill at, developing effective marketing and community engagement campaigns for socially responsible companies. She was subcontracting more and more with freelancers she wished she could hire full time. But she didn't have a place for them to work. Proper office space was obviously what she needed.

The month she moved her business out of the basement was the same month her husband left her. While she was juggling home, child, and business (effectively, she thought), he was even more effectively juggling home, job, and mistress. The affair had been going for several years. They'd been so careful hiding it, no one, including Catherine, had suspected.

It took over eighteen months to negotiate the divorce. Noah was ten by the time it was final, and he was not happy to have his father gone. It showed in his behavior—he acted out at school, let his grades drop, refused to take seriously the detentions he earned. The only thing he did well and regularly was play soccer.

Which left Catherine overseeing the growth of a business, now the main source of income for her and her son, as well as helping Noah come to terms with the divorce. It took a while, but by the time they celebrated his thirteenth birthday, he seemed to have settled into their new life. His grades improved. She stopped getting phone calls about the classes he'd cut.

Now, after what felt like a long time and a lot of work, all parts of her life seemed to have fallen into place. Well, two parts of her life. The third part, a personal life, didn't really exist. Catherine went from home to office and back again in a pattern that hadn't varied in years. Her extracurricular activities were family events with her mom and sisters.

Not that she'd been looking for any sort of serious relationship. She wasn't sure when she'd be ready to trust a man to get that close to her again. But she was beginning to think some male company might be nice. Maybe it was time to take her personal life off the back burner. A pleasant, safe, lobby-and-elevator relationship with the sexiest man in Philly seemed like the perfect way to practice her rusty skills. The ones she'd been using so infrequently she thought he smelled of gingerbread instead of something a little less domestic and a bit more dangerous.

• • •

Thanks to a long and complicated history with women which included a brief marriage in his twenties as well as a relationship in his thirties that had turned out almost as badly, Dominic Russo was a cautious man, but his patience was beginning to wear thin. He couldn't remember when he'd worked as hard to get a response from a woman as he had to get one from Catherine Bennett. Usually, when he showed interest in a woman, she responded in some manner, even if it was to turn him down. Catherine hadn't. She was friendly enough in the elevator, but she didn't react as he expected. She either didn't get the hints he dropped about having lunch with him or she chose to disregard them, although that seemed unlikely. Not that he was vain. Well, *that* vain. He was experienced, however, and knew what it was like to be brushed off. There had been no cold response or quick turndown from Catherine. Hell, the problem was she'd had no reaction at all to his attempts to move their conversation out of the elevator to a table for two in a nice restaurant someplace.

He knew she was seven years younger than he was, but he doubted age was a problem. He didn't think she knew his. He only knew hers because of the paperwork and background check he did on all prospective tenants. He also knew her credit history, where she lived, how old her son was, and what her income had been last year. There were distinct advantages to owning the building and having people work for you who knew how to do a thorough background check.

Among the things he didn't know, however, was whether she had a man in her life other than a son and an ex-husband. Boyfriends didn't show up in the kind of search his management company conducted for a lease agreement.

He'd checked out social media, but that hadn't helped either. The only Facebook page and website he could find connected to her were company pages. So, although he'd never seen her enter or leave the building with anyone but a young boy he assumed was her son, it was possible she had a boyfriend. But if she did, why hadn't she told him when he'd hinted at lunch?

Of course, it was also possible, God help him, he was losing his touch with women. He shuddered at the thought. But he had to face the fact he wasn't a kid anymore. He was forty-five, not thirty. No, he refused to go there. It had to be something else.

With enough time, he'd always been able to charm anyone. It was one of the reasons for his success both with women and in business. He was sure all he had to do was figure out a way to get her in a longer conversation, and he'd be able to persuade her to have lunch. Maybe even dinner.

The most likely place for a conversation was the coffee bar in the building lobby. He knew she went there every morning when she came to work. Occasionally she was there in the afternoon, too. He'd seen her a couple of times when he'd been coming in or going out of the building. All he had to do was figure out when she'd be there in the afternoon, when she'd be more likely to sit and talk, and "accidently" run into her the same way he "accidently" ran into her most mornings in the lobby.

• • •

"Here," Melody said as she handed Catherine a brightly colored envelope. "A bunch of cards for free lattes came from the coffee place downstairs. Nice way to end the week."

"Thanks." Catherine took the envelope and started to put it in her desk drawer. "I'll use it next week."

"Don't put it away. You have to use it today. Between three and four."

"How weird. I've never heard of anything like that."

"It's probably some promo for new tenants. And they want us to use the 'get out of paying' card when they're not too busy. Then if we like their stuff, we'll come back."

"Why would they have to worry about us buying our coffee there? It's five blocks to the next nearest place. Who'd go out in this heat when we can stay in air-conditioned comfort and still get our caffeine fix?"

"Well, then, maybe it's a welcome to the building. Whatever it is, a free latte is a free latte. I was hoping you'd go get one for me as well as for yourself. The ISP guy will be here soon to sort out the glitches in the router system they installed."

"Yeah, we need to get it fixed. It's so unreliable right now it's a pain in the neck. I'm ready to go back to our old provider if they can't make it right."

"Exactly what I told him. So, bring me back a decaf."

• • •

There she was. His deal with the coffee bar owner had worked. Dominic closed his laptop and watched, unobserved, as Catherine made her way from the elevator with two other people from her office to where the barista waited to take their orders. Today, instead of one of her business suits, she was wearing black pants and a cream-colored shirt. A heavy gold chain and gold hoop earrings were the only accessories she wore. Simple, good taste, nothing overdone. Dominic liked simple, good taste.

He also liked the black heels she wore, which must add three, maybe four, inches to her height. No, not liked. Loved. Shoes like that probably hurt like hell to wear, but they sure made some interesting changes to a woman's body and to the way she walked. On Catherine Bennett they looked marvelous, emphasizing a very nice butt and what he knew, from the days she wore skirts, were shapely calves on legs that were long even without the extra inches from her stilettos.

Allowing her colleagues to go first, she finally got to order lattes with two of the cards he'd paid for. The barista looked over Catherine's shoulder at him, and Dominic nodded. Something in the interchange must have caught her attention because she turned and, when she recognized him, acknowledged him with a smile. He waved her over to where he was sitting.

"Did you get one of these mysterious free latte cards, too?" she asked as she approached the table.

"No, I didn't. You must have hit the coffee jackpot today."

"Maybe it's some sort of deal for new tenants. Although if it was, you'd know about it, wouldn't you?"

"Not necessarily." He indicated the chair across the table from him. "Do you have time to join me while I finish my coffee?"

She hesitated for a moment, but when she glanced over at the two people she'd arrived with, they were waving goodbye as they left. "Okay. Sure. I guess I have a few minutes until my lattes are ready."

"So, what's a nice girl like you doing in a place like this?" he asked. "Oh, wait, you already told me. You're here for the free coffee. So maybe the line should be, 'do you come here often?'"

"Do those lines still work? They're awfully old—or at the very least well used." She was smiling, but the sting was still there.

"Ouch. A not-so-subtle reminder either of my impending old age or the rut my creativity is in. Guess I need to up my game to talk to you."

"Sorry, just trying to be funny. But apparently being insulting instead. No offense meant."

"None taken, then." He sipped at his coffee. "Let me try something else. The other day you mentioned having problems with your Internet provider. Have you gotten them taken care of?"

"Not really. I hope when I get back upstairs the service guy will be there to get it fixed."

"Want some help? The provider you mentioned does a lot of business in this building, and I could probably get their attention pretty quickly."

"If this doesn't get it taken care of, I may accept your offer. It's been the only glitch in our move. I guess I should be happy things have gone so smoothly, but this one rather important detail is making me crazy. And it's screwing up my weekend. I'd hoped to get out early today, but with this still unresolved, I want to hang around until I'm sure it's straightened out."

Trying to sound casual, even though he was intensely interested, he took the chance to find out if she had a boyfriend. "Hot date?"

She snorted. "Hardly. Family obligation. A sister's birthday."

"Your family live in the city?" He hoped the relief he felt wasn't evident in his voice.

"Sisters live in the suburbs but my mom still lives in South Philly, in the middle of the old Italian neighborhood where I grew up."

"Right. I keep forgetting you're Italian. Bennett sounds so WASP-y."

"How do you know I'm Italian?" She frowned.

"I assumed Alessandro—your middle name—is your birth name or a family name of some sort, and it sounds pretty Italian. Don't forget, I'm your landlord. I know quite a bit about you."

"I'm not sure whether to be creeped out, complimented, or impressed."

"Let's go with complimented and impressed. I like the sound of it better than creeped out." He finished his coffee and crushed the paper cup. "Are you complimented enough to have lunch with me sometime next week so we can continue this conversation?"

"That's kind of you, but I don't really go out socially, and besides, you're not only my landlord but my competition."

"If I promised it wouldn't be about your lease, could I change your mind?"

She stood and picked up the coffee the barista had delivered to her. "Still not a good idea. But thank you. I'm flattered." Without saying anything further, she headed to the elevator.

• • •

Catherine was relieved when Dominic didn't immediately follow her. Being in the closed space of an elevator car with him after turning down his invitation for lunch would have been uncomfortable to say the least. Especially since it must have been obvious she hadn't even given his suggestion a second thought.

She'd discounted the oblique references he'd made about having lunch, thinking he was joking. But now it seemed she should have paid closer attention. He'd really asked her out. Or maybe not *out*. Maybe lunch in the deli next to the coffee shop. But to lunch, at least.

Part of her was pleased he'd asked. It had been a long time since she'd been the object of a man's attention for anything other than business. And she'd caught the attention of someone who was more than a run-of-the-mill guy. Dominic Russo was so far out of her league she couldn't see even the Class A division of his league from where she stood.

Part of her was puzzled. Why would Mister Sex on Legs be interested in her? If they'd been bicycles, he'd be a titanium racing bike and she would be an old Schwinn, the kind with training wheels, not exactly his usual speed.

But most of her reaction was determination never to put herself in the position of being hurt like she'd been by the disastrous end of her marriage. Surely, given who he was, Dominic would tire of her even more quickly than her ex-husband had and leave. She was not about to set herself up for *that* again.

Wait. He was also in the same industry. Maybe he wanted to talk about a business opportunity for her firm. Oh, shit. She'd jumped to the wrong conclusion. Of course it wasn't personal. He wouldn't be interested in her. Suppose she'd just been stupid enough to turn down a chance to work with The Russo Group. Pissing off the man who was both her landlord and the founder of the biggest communications firm in the city was not a good business decision. Working with them could be the making of her company.

No, if it had been business, he would have said something like, "I have a business proposition I'd like to talk about with you," wouldn't he? She wasn't *that* much out of practice with men that she'd miss a business opportunity. It was personal, all right. But why would he ask her out? If the rumors Melody kept telling her about were true, he could have any woman—had probably *had* most of the women—in Philly. Why her?

Then the most likely reason occurred. Suppose the "why" was neither a personal invitation nor a chance to work with him. Suppose flattering her with his attention and a bit of lunch was his way of pumping her for information about her business? Maybe she was getting a little too successful for his comfort and he wanted a chance to evaluate how much of a threat she was to his business. That day in her office, he'd said he'd been watching how successful she'd become in the industry.

Damn. Damn. Damn. How could she figure out why he'd asked?

She was still mulling it all over when she heard Melody say, "Catherine? Are you okay?" after which the door to the elevator began to close. She'd been so caught up with worrying about what she might have done, she hadn't felt the elevator stop or seen the door open. Before she could hit the button to stop the door from closing, the car returned to the lobby. This time when the door opened, Dominic got in. *Why is he still here, and where are the other elevators when you need them?*

He smiled as if unsurprised to see her, and she felt herself flush what was, she was sure, a bright shade of pink. Leaning in front of her to press the button for his floor, he raised his eyebrows. "Lost?"

"Not exactly. I must have pushed the wrong button. Sometimes it happens when my hands are full." She indicated the two cups she was carrying. She knew that wouldn't explain why she'd gone up and come back down, but it was the best she could do.

"Let me." He punched the button for the tenth floor. "Wouldn't want you to waste your afternoon wandering around in the elevator shaft."

"Thanks." She was sure she'd now moved from bright pink to deep red. The tenth floor couldn't come soon enough.

Chapter 3

A ruby red rose bud, with no thorns, in a clear glass bud vase arrived at the Bennett and Associates office early Monday morning. There was no card with it—only a routing slip saying it was for Catherine. Melody rang the florist named on the paperwork, but the woman who answered said it was from someone who wished to remain anonymous.

For a few seconds after Mel conveyed the message, Catherine wondered if Dominic Russo was the *someone*. But she dismissed the idea. Why would he send her flowers—ah, *a* flower? She'd turned him down for lunch, not gone out with him. More likely it was an apology from her sister for picking a fight with her at the family birthday party on Friday. Nothing so simple as a phone call and an "I'm sorry" from Mary Ellen. Well, she deserved to fume for a day or two before Catherine acknowledged the peace offering.

A second vase was delivered on Tuesday morning with two yellow roses in it. Again, there was no card. Melody once again called the florist and once again was told they couldn't reveal the name of the person sending the flowers. Odd, Catherine thought, that her sister would choose to apologize like this.

Four peach-colored, sweetly scented roses showed up on Wednesday. This time there was a card, which said only "Please?" Before she could stop it, Dominic's name rose to the surface of her mind. Could he be doing this to try and get her to have lunch? No, too absurd. No one wanted lunch with her that badly. It would be nice to think someone like him wanted to spend time with her badly enough to mount a campaign of flowers, but it was unlikely.

It had to be her sister being clever. But when she broke down and called Mary Ellen, Catherine got an apology for the fight they'd had and a snorty laugh when she suggested her sister had sent three vases of roses.

By the time eight white roses with red-edged petals were delivered on Thursday, Melody had Googled the meaning of roses and discovered a single rose with no thorns meant "I hope." Yellow roses represented "a new beginning," peach roses, "let's get together." And white roses edged in red, "togetherness." Catherine told her to stop wasting her time. But when she was alone, she remembered the card with the peach roses, the ones meaning "let's get together," had said "please."

Her staff was enjoying the mystery. A pool had been started laying odds on who was sending the flowers and how long it would take for him—they were sure it was a man—to reveal himself. The bettors were split three ways on who Catherine's secret admirer could be. The first candidate was Jamie Foster, who freelanced for them as a copy editor and always seemed to be flirting with Catherine. The second was Pete Turner, a client who had been very attentive to her when they'd been working on his firm's branding and social media campaign. The last was Dominic. Catherine dismissed with a wave of her hand the idea any of those three men would be interested in her. Two of them she hadn't had any contact with in weeks. The third had stopped showing up in the mornings for their daily ride in the elevator, annoyed, she imagined, that she'd turned him down for lunch.

She did suggest, if her employees had enough money to waste on frivolous bets, she was paying them too much.

The sixteen coral roses ("desire," Melody informed Catherine) that arrived on Friday afternoon were cardless again, leaving Catherine the weekend to wonder who in the world was doing this. She hoped she could stop obsessing about it by burying herself in work as she usually did when Noah was with his father, which was the case this weekend.

On the Saturdays she worked, Catherine walked from her home in University City to the office. On this particular Saturday, it felt good to be out, even though the air was already warm and predicted to be warmer still by the afternoon.

Waiting for the light to change so she could cross the street to her building, she saw Dominic striding toward the front door. She watched from a safe distance, dawdling on the corner, pretending to glance at the offerings in the newspaper kiosk instead of what she was really doing—gawking at Dominic.

After waiting for what she thought was enough time for him to get to his floor, she made her way to the building. But she'd miscalculated. He was coming away from the coffee counter as she walked through the door.

"Morning, Catherine," he said as he punched the "up" button.

"Good morning." She didn't meet his eyes, for the first time nervous about being in the elevator with him alone. Although she didn't know why.

Before she could sort it out, the man at the security desk interrupted. "I have a delivery for you, Ms. Bennett," he said as he handed her a large box with green florist paper stapled around what she knew would be more roses. She took the package, wondering how the hell the person sending the flowers knew she worked on Saturdays.

Dominic held the elevator door for her to enter. "An admirer?" he asked.

"Something like that," she muttered, not wanting to answer any questions about the package in her arms. The ten-floor ride to her office was shaping up to be as long as a covered wagon journey to the uncharted west. She was saved at the last minute when Dominic's creative director, Edie Martin, joined them, barely avoiding being hit by the closing doors. She smiled warmly at Dominic and gave a perfunctory "hello" to Catherine. On the ride to the tenth floor, Edie kept Dominic occupied with mundane office chatter, much to Catherine's relief.

Exiting the elevator on her floor felt like she was escaping from an atmosphere overly charged with—with something. She wasn't sure what.

Once inside her office, she placed the box on her desk. She didn't have to rip off the paper to know what was inside. The only thing she didn't know was what color the thirty-two roses would be.

They were blush pink, stunningly beautiful, gently perfumed, and without a card. Once more she felt either treasured or stalked. She wasn't sure which.

She didn't get much work accomplished. Silently watching her from most of the level surfaces in her office were different sized containers holding a total of sixty-three roses—she'd counted several times—in a variety of colors and various stages of bloom. They seemed to be asking her a question she couldn't answer.

Catherine holed up in her house on Sunday and stayed in her robe until after lunch. But not one of the books she tried to read held her attention for more than a few pages. Even the comics in the newspaper were too hard to follow.

If only she could figure out who was sending the damn roses.

She came back to the same thought every time she ran the puzzle around in her mind. It took someone with a lot of spare cash to pull off this stunt.

Maybe her staff was right—Pete Turner had been awfully attentive when they'd worked with him. And he had called her directly at least three or four times since they'd completed their contract with him to ask what seemed to be minor questions and to chat with her. His start-up firm was doing very well in the high-tech field; he could afford all the flowers. But why would he do something like this? Wouldn't he come right out and ask her for a date?

And Jamie Foster. He'd had coffee with her a couple times—always, she'd assumed, for business reasons. He made her laugh, and he flirted with her relentlessly in his cute, redheaded Irish way when he was in the office. Of course, he flirted with anyone who had XX chromosomes, but he dated copywriters from her shop who were a lot closer to his twenty-something age than she was. Besides, she doubted a freelancer would have the money it took for this stunt.

Which led her back to Dominic. The betting pool among her staff had moved heavily in his direction, Melody said, for two reasons. First, he could afford it, and second, several of them had been in the elevator with their boss and their landlord and swore they could feel the heat the two of them generated just standing next to each other.

Catherine had to agree Dominic was one of the few people she knew who had the kind of money it took to buy all those expensive flowers. What she didn't see was why he'd do it. It didn't make sense. He'd asked her out; she'd turned him down. A man with his ego would ask again. Or go on to the next woman. Wouldn't he?

The only other possibility she could think of was someone wanted a job with her firm and was trying to show off their creativity. She'd had all sorts of things delivered to her from potential employees trying to demonstrate their abilities—haiku poems attached to a balloon bouquet, a complete marketing campaign for an imaginary firm, each stage inside a nested box and tied up with red ribbons, banners on posts across the tiny front lawn of her house with the man's credentials outlined on the banners. (That one had frightened her, driving her to consult an old family friend in the police department.)

But if it were a job hunter, why wouldn't he—she—identify him/herself? And if they were looking for a job, would they have the kind of money it would take to pull off this trick? She'd have to remember to go through the file of unsolicited CVs she'd received to see if maybe there was a way to connect the flowers with one of them—someone named Rose? Or Flowers?

Maybe it was her family belatedly celebrating her new office space and the success of her business. Nah, that was easy to dismiss. No one in her family would ever spend that kind of money on flowers. Dinner at a good restaurant, yes. Flowers, no.

And who would have a reason to include a card saying "Please?"

Which brought her back to Dominic. Again. Damn it to hell, if he was behind this, why wouldn't he just call and put her out of her misery? She was tired of waiting for an end to the campaign but not about to confront him in case she was wrong. How humiliating would that be?

Obsessed with trying to solve the rose mystery, she hadn't gotten nearly enough work done over the weekend. Which left so much to accomplish on Monday, she was able to forget about roses for a while. Until she took a quick break for something to eat and realized there had been no more delivered yet. Maybe, she decided, her run of roses was over without any explanation of what it had all been about. She wasn't sure if she was relieved or disappointed, although she was happy to be able to finally concentrate on work.

Focusing on her computer, she didn't hear Melody come into her office later that afternoon until her office administrator cleared her throat. When she looked up, Catherine's heart sank. Or maybe sang.

"Your daily delivery of roses has arrived," Melody said. "It's late this time. I'd almost given up." She had a huge package on a cart. "You better figure out what the hell's going on. This thing weighs a ton, and if your mysterious admirer keeps it up, doubling today's haul means …"

"I know, I know. Tomorrow one hundred and twenty eight roses." She motioned toward the small conference table in her office. "Put them over there."

Melody rolled the cart to the table. As she went out the door she said, "Oh, there's a card this time. Maybe it'll help."

A card. Catherine whacked her leg on the corner of her desk in her eagerness to get to the flowers. As she unpinned the envelope from the paper around the flowers, her hand trembled slightly. Before she opened it, she ripped off the tissue paper revealing a vase holding roses of every color in the rose world. Then she opened the envelope and removed the card.

There was still no name. But the note said, "It's only lunch."

It *had* been Dominic. He wanted to have lunch with her, and it certainly didn't seem to be about business.

She yelped, "That's it!"

"What's wrong? What happened?" Melody asked as she burst into the room a moment later.

"Sorry, I didn't mean to frighten you. Look." Catherine passed the card to Melody.

Mel read the card then handed it back to her, a puzzled look on her face. "Is this supposed to mean something?"

"I turned Dominic Russo down for lunch a week or so ago. I think he's been sending the roses to get me to change my mind."

Melody whistled softly. "Holy crap. First of all, why the hell would you turn him down? Second, the man must really want to have lunch with you to spend this much money on flowers. Third, wow. Just wow."

"I turned him down because … well, for lots of reasons. I was flattered, of course, but I was puzzled and I ..."

"You were scared," Melody said.

"Not scared. Reluctant. I had no idea why he asked me to have lunch. If it was personal, I wasn't sure after all these years of no social life that I wanted to start up again by jumping into the deep end of the big-boy dating pool. Not to mention set myself up for a bruised ego when he dumped me, which he was bound to do. And if it wasn't personal, I knew I didn't want him to be all charming over a sandwich while he pumped me for information about my business." She tapped the card on the table as she spoke. "I still don't know what he's up to, but I have to do something about this. It's distracting everyone in the office."

"Distracting you, don't you mean?" Melody said. "We're all having a good time *and* getting our work done. You're the one who's been sidetracked by the attack of the killer roses."

Ignoring her friend, Catherine went on, "Are any of those big boxes left from our move? I have an idea how to make this stop."

"Stop? Why? This is no plot to pick your brain. Not with all the money he spent on flowers. The man wants to have lunch with you. So go to lunch. Are you sure you want to chase him away?"

"I'm positive. I can't risk it."

"Okay, but I think you're nuts." Melody sighed and shrugged. "There are a couple boxes left. Want me to get one?"

"Better make it two."

Chapter 4

Ten minutes later, Catherine pushed a cart crammed with vases of roses into the reception area of The Russo Group offices. An attractive fifty-something woman with white hair and a warm smile asked, "Can I help you?"

"I'm Catherine Bennett. I'm here to see Dominic."

"Do you have an appointment?"

"No, I don't. It's not business. It's personal. Would you tell me where his office is, please?"

The warmth in her smile began to wane. "Why don't you put your cart over here while I see if he's in. I think he might be in a meeting."

"Thanks, that's okay. I'll deliver these myself."

The woman picked up a telephone, probably to warn her boss there was a crazy lady at the reception desk with a cart full of flowers, which could very possibly be more dangerous than it looked. But Catherine was determined. She started toward the hall, intending to knock on every door until she found Dominic. Then she heard his voice and, ignoring the frantic waving of the woman on the phone, went toward the sound.

He was outside a corner office, talking to his creative director. When he saw Catherine wheeling the cart toward him, he smiled. "Ms. Bennett. How nice to see you." He dismissed Edie, saying, "Send the copy to me. I'll take a look at it and let you know what I think." Edie left after glaring at Catherine in a very unfriendly manner.

"Come in. My office is just here." He stepped aside so she could enter a large room with two walls of floor-to-ceiling windows. One window looked out on the street the building fronted. The other framed the Parkway, leading to the best view of the Art Museum

Catherine had seen outside a guidebook or a *Rocky* movie. Posters featuring some of The Russo Group's award-winning campaigns covered the other two walls. A large leather couch and low table were in front of the glass wall overlooking the street. In the center of the room, slanted to take advantage of the museum view, was an oversized desk shaped like a boomerang—no corners, only soft, sensuous curves in a wood so dark chocolate in color it looked good enough to eat.

Only Dominic Russo, Catherine thought, would have a desk that made an observer think of sex and chocolate.

"What can I do for you, Catherine?" Dominic asked, a smile flickering across his mouth as if he were trying hard not to let it take over his face.

"I want to know what all this is." She waved her hand over the cart.

"It appears to be several boxes full of vases and flowers."

"I know that, Dominic. I don't know why."

"Why what?"

She ran her fingers through her hair in frustration. "Stop playing games. Tell me why you've been sending me roses every day."

"I thought the note was clear. I want to have lunch with you."

"This … response, or whatever it is … seems out of proportion to extending a simple lunch invitation, doesn't it?"

"I confess I expected you to catch on before we got to sixty-four roses, so perhaps it is. But I don't give up when I want something. And I want to have lunch with you."

"Why?"

"You're a very attractive woman. Some people think I'm an attractive man. We seem to enjoy talking to each other, and we both eat lunch on occasion. Why not?"

"I told you. I don't do social things. And it feels odd. You're my landlord. We compete for the same work."

"I promise we won't talk about the building, your lease, or our work. And everyone needs a personal life. Even you, Catherine."

"It isn't going to happen, Dominic. It just isn't." She pushed the cart across the room to his desk. "I'm leaving the roses here. You can do whatever you want with them. Call after you take care of the flowers, and I'll send someone to retrieve the cart. And please stop sending them."

"As I said, I don't give up when I want something. The florist will double the number of roses arriving every day at your office until I call him and say you've agreed to have lunch with me. Tomorrow will be ..."

"One hundred and twenty-eight. I can do the math."

"Even as we speak there are young girls in some Central American country packing up the flowers they've clipped and made pretty for you. You've probably been responsible for a shortage of roses in the Mid-Atlantic region or at least in Center City Philadelphia because ..."

"Stop." She closed her eyes for a few seconds and took a breath or two to clear her head. "Okay. Lunch tomorrow. Downstairs in the deli."

"Friday. I'll meet you in the lobby at eleven thirty, and we'll drive to the place I have in mind. It's not within walking distance."

"Why would I agree to that?"

"You've already agreed in principle. Now we're settling the details." When she hesitated, he added, "Keep in mind, one hundred twenty eight tomorrow and two hundred fifty six the day after."

Her shoulders sagged in defeat. "Friday, then. Eleven thirty."

He escorted her to the hall. "I'm looking forward to it, Catherine."

She could have sworn he was about to lean down and kiss her but pulled back at the last minute. Or maybe it was her imagination.

• • •

Thank God the mystery of the roses was solved, because it ended up being the workweek from hell. Catherine needed all her focus to get everything done—a complicated response to a request for proposals for a potential project, an unexpected chance to submit qualifications to a new client, and the kick-off of a major public involvement campaign, on top of the usual workload for retained clients.

By the end of the week, when all the deadlines had been met, Catherine was actually glad she had a lunch outside the office. She'd have a pleasant meal with Dominic, a break for an hour or so, then come back refreshed so she could sort out her office. All week, she'd had little chance to clean up from a meeting about one project before she'd had the next group of people come in to talk about another one. The evidence was strewn around her small conference table, the couch, and her desk. She hated to work in clutter and needed to get it taken care of.

When she came into the office on Friday morning, Melody greeted her with a knowing smile and a raised eyebrow. "You don't often wear a dress to work. What's this all about? As if I didn't know."

"Summer's almost over and I haven't worn this yet. It seemed like a good day for it." Catherine smoothed imaginary wrinkles out of the beige pencil dress she wore then tugged the edge of the v-neckline up to make sure there wasn't too much décolletage showing.

She'd brushed out her hair after her shower and left it loose instead of pulling it back in a low ponytail or twisting it into a soft bun, as she usually did. The dark brown platform sandals she wore matched the narrow belt around her waist. A thin gold chain, small hoop earrings, and coordinating gold bangle bracelet completed the look.

"Yeah, right. Airing out the dress." Melody shook her head in disbelief. "Fess up. You wore it because you're going on a lunch date with Mister Sex on Legs."

"How do you know who I'm having lunch with?"

"Half the people in the building know. Dominic's assistant said it's the talk of their office. They got to take home all your roses, by the way, which annoyed me. I would have thought you'd save at least one vase for me."

Catherine had never thought about who might know about the lunch. Of course, more than a few of Dominic's staff had seen her walk in with the cart and out without it. May have even heard their conversation. He hadn't shut the door to his office while they talked, which, at the time, she'd thought was a good idea. Now she wasn't so sure.

"Okay, yes, I'm having lunch with him today. It was the only way I could get him to stop sending roses. He's quite determined when he's after something, apparently."

"Obviously what he's after is you." Melody was all-out grinning now. "Don't hurry back. Everything we had to get out is out. And everything that needed your okay has been okayed."

"He's meeting me in the lobby at eleven thirty, so I'm sure I'll be back by one."

"Only if you're very unlucky. And I have a strong feeling today is *not* your unlucky day. Besides, I won the pool, and I'm blowing it on lunch with a cute guy. If you're out for a long lunch, I can be, too."

Catherine started toward her office, then halted, her back to Melody. "Okay, my curiosity's killing me. How much did you win?"

"A dollar for every rose. I bet on Dominic and sixty-four."

Muttering, "I need to hire a staff with more respect for me," Catherine stormed down the hall to her office with Melody's laughter in her ears.

Chapter 5

At eleven twenty, Catherine punched the button for the elevator. A few minutes later, the door opened, and there he was, Mister Sex on Legs himself, grinning and holding out his hand as if he were welcoming her to his personal elevator. Okay, he owned the building, so in a way it *was* his personal elevator.

And what was with his clothes? He was wearing a navy blazer with tan pants and a white shirt with no tie. The top two buttons of the shirt were undone, and the merest hint of dark chest hair peeked out. It was the most informal she'd ever seen him during the workweek. What was he up to? And why was she even noticing his chest hair?

"Ready for lunch, Ms. Bennett?" he asked.

Ignoring his hand, she walked to the opposite corner of the elevator then scolded herself mentally. The man didn't have to be avoided as though he were nuclear waste. Although, come to think of it, he might be as dangerous.

"As long as there are no roses involved, I guess I'm ready. I think I'm off that particular flower for a year or ten."

"I'll make a note to remind myself to send something else the next time."

She wasn't sure if he was in a good mood or making fun of her. She decided to believe it was a good mood. "I trust by agreeing to this lunch I've put an end to your need to inundate me with flowers."

"My goal is to put an end to your resistance to spending time with me. I can go either way with the flowers."

"Remember, I said I don't have a social life. I'm looking at this as a business opportunity."

"Really? I'm not. It's definitely personal. I hope I can change your mind about that, too. I can be very persuasive."

"I'm sure you can. But I'm hard to convince."

By this time, the elevator had reached the lobby. She was happy to be out of the enclosed space that seemed to have heated up considerably in the time it took to descend ten floors, thanks to the damn late summer weather. Or something.

Dominic waved her out ahead of him, followed her to the building exit, and, reaching around her, pushed open the door for her. She could have sworn she felt more heat. Weather again. What else could it be?

Sitting at the curb was a black Cadillac Escalade with smoked windows. Dominic said, "Here's our ride," and surprised her by opening the back passenger door for her. When she climbed in, she got a second surprise. There was a driver in the front. Dominic made the introductions when he joined her in the back seat and added, "We're good to go, Jack."

Jack smoothly inserted the vehicle into the traffic moving toward Broad Street.

Catherine glanced back and forth from the driver to her lunch date several times before saying, "A driver? A bit extravagant, isn't it?"

"Not according to the Philadelphia police and my insurance company. I got so many tickets, they both suggested I find another way to transport myself. Even with benefits, Jack's cheaper than paying the fines and the increased premiums."

"Are you really such a bad driver?" Catherine asked.

"I'm not a bad driver. I'm a very fast driver. And a major illegal parker. In fact, the last judge I appealed to in the futile attempt to have the fine reduced said I might hold the all-time record for illegal parking. Apparently I've been ticketed at least twice in every possible illegal spot in the city." He sounded almost proud.

"You drive fast in this behemoth?"

"No, I have a Maserati." This time he was definitely proud.

"Ah, I'd probably drive fast if I had one of those, too."

"I'd like to see that. Maybe I'll let you get the chance to show me sometime."

At Dominic's request Jack touched a view screen and the sound of a man singing filled the vehicle. It was *Norma*, and maybe Pavarotti, Catherine thought.

"If you don't like opera," Dominic said, "we can listen to something else."

"I grew up in an Italian home. Of course I like opera."

"Who's your favorite composer?"

A discussion of the virtues of the two great Italian composers, Verdi and Puccini, ensued, with Dominic defending Puccini and Catherine taking Verdi's side.

Caught up in the conversation and the music, she hadn't paid attention to where they were going until she glanced out the window and was startled by what she saw. "We're on the Walt Whitman Bridge. Where are you taking me?"

"To a small seafood restaurant I like. A business acquaintance of mine owns it. I thought it would be nice to have lunch there. I'm sure you'll like it."

"And this restaurant is located where, exactly?"

"Brigantine."

"As in the Jersey Shore?"

"I'm not aware there's a Brigantine any place else."

She wasn't sure whether she was outraged or amused by his presumption. "I can't go down the shore for lunch. I have work to do. My staff will wonder where I am."

"Melody said you've been working twelve-hour days for a couple weeks, which meant they had to work twelve-hour days. You need a break and so does your staff. She knows you won't be back until late this afternoon."

"How do you know what Melody says—or knows?"

"I talked to her yesterday and again today before I left my office."

Now Catherine was sure what she was, and it was outraged. "I'll kill her."

"No, you won't. You'll thank her for being an understanding friend and loyal employee."

"What did you promise her, Russo?"

"I said we'd bring her back a box of saltwater taffy."

"I had no idea she could be bought off so easily. I'm going to have to rethink how much I tell her about my business operations." She tapped the driver on the shoulder. "Jack, I need to get back to my office. Would you mind turning around and dropping me off? Then you can take Dominic wherever the hell he wants to go. Or you can rearrange the words in that sentence and take him there."

Jack's shaking shoulders indicated he was stifling a laugh. Dominic didn't bother to hide his amusement. "Do you really think you can convince my driver to do what you want when I've asked him to take us to Brigantine? You're a beautiful woman, which probably means most men do what you ask, but I don't think it'll trump the salary I pay him." He looked up and seemed to catch his driver's eye in the rearview mirror. "Right, Jack?"

"Whatever you say, Dominic. At least this time."

"I'll have you charged as an accessory to kidnapping when I report your boss to the police, Jack," Catherine said.

Jack laughed. "If Dominic hasn't gotten me in trouble, Ms. Bennett, I don't think you can."

Dominic was clearly enjoying her reaction as well as his driver's responses. "Catherine, relax. Your staff has known about this since yesterday. They know where I'm taking you and how long we'll be gone. No one's kidnapping you. If you have to have a motive behind it other than my wanting to have lunch with you, think of it as a way to help a restaurant trying to claw its way back to life after Hurricane Sandy."

"Guilt? Now you're using guilt?"

"I assume you were raised Catholic. Guilt usually works on those of us who were." He was grinning at her still.

She shook her head. "You're like a freight train. You don't stop when you have a goal in mind, do you?"

"I told you. When I go after something I want, I get it."

"Then explain to me why you want to have lunch with me so badly."

"Excellent. Let's talk about you. But first …"

From a small ice chest by his feet, Dominic extracted a bottle of sparkling wine. Two glasses followed. He popped the cork with a deft twist, poured the wine, and offered a glass to Catherine. She hesitated for a few seconds, finally taking the glass although she held it away from her body as if not sure what it was.

"It's just prosecco, Catherine. No magic potion; no drugs." He raised his glass, touched it to hers, and said, "*Salute*. To getting to know each other better."

She watched him sip from the glass for a few seconds before drinking from hers and finally relaxing back against the soft leather seat. "Okay, I guess I might as well play your game. I seem to be stuck with you for the afternoon."

Jack muffled another laugh.

"Be quiet, Jack. If you can't help me, the least you can do is not laugh at me." She turned to her host. "And you, Dominic, you haven't answered my question yet. Why do you want to have lunch with me?"

"I've wanted to meet you socially since your presentation to the business roundtable. You intrigued me. You were smart and very professional, all in one quite lovely package. I like brains in a woman, particularly a beautiful one. And you've put a new spin on a business I was sure I knew everything about, which also interested me. But I could never figure a way to meet you. I couldn't remember seeing you at the events I'm forced to attend in the name of business."

He made a face that might be disgust for what he had to do for his work. How he managed to make disgust look sexy Catherine didn't know, but he did.

He went on, "I'd see you sometimes when our firms were both pitching the same potential client, but that was clearly not the right time to strike up a personal conversation. And I hesitated to track you down at home, assuming you might not appreciate being cold called by someone you'd barely met. So, when you leased space in the building ..."

"You mean, leased space in *your* building."

Continuing as though she hadn't spoken, he said, "... leased space in the building, I decided it was my opportunity to get to know you. It took a little more effort and time than I expected, but here we are. Finally."

He topped off their glasses. "You fascinate me, Catherine Alessandro Bennett. The Italian woman with the WASP name. The founder and creative brains behind Philly's up-and-coming strategic communications firm who gets her clients without making the rounds of every boring social event in the city. Who turns down political work so she can work with companies on strategic plans that include political activities ..."

"I thought we weren't going to discuss business."

"I'm not discussing business. I'm telling you why you fascinate me. You're not like any other woman I've ever met. So I wanted to have lunch with you. To get to know who this interesting woman is."

By this time, Catherine had kicked off her sandals and rearranged her seat belt so she could tuck her feet under her. Listening to Dominic extoll her virtues, she was sorry she'd ever asked him the question, because he was embarrassing her. Fortunately, he seemed to have run out of compliments for the moment because he changed the subject.

"Now," he said. "It's your turn. Why did you decide to have lunch with me?"

"So there would be a few roses left in the Western Hemisphere for some other egomaniacal man to send to the object of his dastardly schemes."

He watched her over the rim of his glass. "That's not true and we both know it."

She blushed but tried to bluff it through. "I don't know what you mean."

"Please, Catherine, give me some credit. I see you almost every day and know how you dress. In the time you've been in the building, you've worn suits or pants, jeans when you work on the weekends, but I've never seen you wear a dress. And you always wear your hair up or tied back, not loose, like now."

He reached over, picked up a strand of hair that had fallen over her shoulder into the V of her neckline, and twisted it around his finger as if to memorize its texture. As he did, the back of his hand brushed her collarbone, making her shiver. Her skin tingled even in places he hadn't touched. She swore even her hair reacted.

After he'd tucked the lock of hair behind her ear, he lingered for a moment, drawing his fingers down the side of her face. "You dressed like this for lunch with me. Why would you make the effort if you didn't want to be here?"

Damn it. She was cornered. He'd figured out in no time what she'd refused to admit to herself until that morning as she got ready—she very much wanted to have lunch with him and had dressed carefully for it.

"Well," she began, not meeting his eyes. "I thought maybe we'd be going to some upscale place, so a dress seemed appropriate."

"Has anyone ever told you what a bad liar you are?"

"Yes, sadly." She sighed. "I wasn't called St. Catherine in high school for no reason."

"Is being bad at lying the only reason?"

"No. There were others." She finished off the glass of wine. "But it takes more than a glass of bubbly and a drive to Jersey to find out what they were."

"I'll look forward to figuring it out, then." He topped off their glasses again and changed the subject.

The drive to Brigantine went by quickly. In what seemed like only a few minutes, Dominic's driver announced they'd reached their destination—Sergio's.

The Sergio in the name of the restaurant greeted them personally, fussing over Dominic like a close relative or a long-lost friend, seating them at a table with a view of the beach and the people enjoying the sun and surf. The lunch, as promised by Dominic, was delicious. After a green salad and a basket of crusty bread, they were served the best cioppino Catherine had ever had, accompanied by a glass of a crisp Soave.

Sergio didn't allow anyone else near them. He served the food, bused the table, even brought out a second linen napkin so Catherine could protect her dress from the spicy tomato sauce she might accidently splash on it.

Dominic and Catherine spent almost two hours eating, talking, laughing. She was pleasantly surprised by how much she enjoyed his company and how easily the conversation between them flowed. Each found out where the other had gone to school—Yale for Dominic, Penn State for Catherine—and what their families had been like when they grew up—loud, noisy, and full of love in both cases. They had both spent time at the Jersey Shore when they were kids, she in Wildwood, he on Long Beach Island. There was no discussion of business.

But it was when Dominic excused himself to take a phone call that Catherine learned the most interesting thing about him from Sergio.

While Dominic picked up a take-out order for his driver, Jack brought the Escalade to the front door of the restaurant where

Catherine joined him. She hopped in the back seat and took the opportunity to text Melody, asking what was going on at the office. The immediate return message said nothing required her to hurry back.

"So," Dominic said, as he joined her in the back of the SUV, "did Melody reassure you about how things were going?"

"How did you know? And they're fine. I assume when you talked to whoever called you, you found out the same about your office."

"It was Edie with a question that could have waited until I got back, but yes, everything's good there, too."

Curious about the woman she'd seen many times now without ever feeling any warmth from her, Catherine asked, "Have you and Edie worked together long?"

"Ten, twelve years. She worked her way up from copywriter to creative director."

She hesitated about asking the question she had, even if the answer might solve the mystery of Edie's attitude toward her. But she decided what the hell, and asked anyway. "Have you ever dated her?"

"Why would you ask that?" He looked genuinely perplexed at her question.

"She seems very possessive of you. Particularly when you're talking to a woman." *Talking to me, for example.*

"I think you're imagining something not there. She's just loyal to my firm. And before you ask the same question about anyone else who works for me, I subscribe to the principle that it's bad form to dip your pen in company ink. But I'd rather talk about something more interesting than my HR policies. What did you think of lunch?"

"It was wonderful and Sergio is delightful." She smiled. "He's also very revealing."

"Now what could Sergio reveal to you to put that cat-lapping-up-cream expression on your face?"

"Well, I tried to pay for lunch while you were on the phone and ..."

"You did what? Are you trying to insult me?" His fake anger was amusing. "My God, woman, you could have had a terrible effect on my feelings of self-worth."

"I doubt it. But he wouldn't let me pay anyway."

"And you found out he won't let me pay either, I assume."

"Yes, because DR Investments Limited owns the whole row of shops and restaurants where his place is. You loaned every one of the owners interest free money to rebuild after Hurricane Sandy. Which explains why their block looks like it's completely recovered when the buildings on either side are still being renovated."

"Don't make me out to be joining you in sainthood, Catherine. It was a way of protecting my investment."

"No it wasn't. It was because you're a good guy." She was indignant that he wouldn't take credit for what he'd done.

"And this surprises you, does it?"

Catherine rushed to explain, afraid she'd insulted him. "No, not exactly. But it doesn't fit the image I have of the powerful and influential Dominic Russo. I assumed you were the kind of man who makes his money by ..." She struggled to come up with an appropriate word to describe what she thought.

"Screwing over everyone he does business with?"

"More like someone for whom profitability is the only goal."

"Catherine, I haven't gotten as far as I have by being a nasty son of a bitch who merely wants to make a buck. I hire talented staff and pay them well; I only work for clients I believe in, and insist on good work even if we sometimes lose money on the contract. I like to sleep well at night and be proud of what my company does."

"Did you choose where we had lunch because you wanted me to find out what you'd done for the owners of those shops?"

"No, I chose it because it was far enough away to give us time together in the car and a good meal when we got there."

"And you didn't think Sergio would tell me what a good guy you are?"

"So now I'm not only a ruthless businessman, I'm someone who would use another person you perceive to be in my debt to get you to like me personally."

"It's possible you'd do something like that to influence my opinion of you. You do have quite a reputation with women."

"Really? Who knew?"

She rolled her eyes at his disingenuous questions. "You've supposedly left a string of broken hearts from Hoboken to Harrisburg. Which is what happens when you go out with dozens of woman but never more than once or twice with any of them. And haven't you been voted most eligible bachelor in Philly a couple times?"

"Three, but what does that have to do with it?"

"Just that you have, like I said, a reputation with women. And maybe you're used to doing whatever it takes to impress them."

"I like women. I won't deny it. But I don't use other people to impress them. Never had to. Not that I'm bragging or anything."

"Right. Not that you're bragging." Another eye roll accompanied her comment.

"You can stop rolling your eyes at me, Catherine. Most of my dates aren't social, they're business. The work my staff does impresses the women I take to dinner. I don't break hearts. I make business deals."

"Are you kidding?"

"No, but if you don't believe me, ask Jack."

"Is he serious, Jack?"

"Yes, ma'am. It's beyond me how he's gotten the rep he has. Unless he has another life with another driver, he's telling the truth. Just business, like he said."

"And how come you know all this gossip, anyway?" Dominic asked. "You did more due diligence on me than on the office building you were about to move into."

"It's not me. It's your mole. Melody has provided me with a multitude of details about you since we've moved into the building. I think she has a crush on you."

"Melody. Damn. We forgot the salt water taffy." He touched Jack's shoulder. "Where's the nearest place we can get saltwater taffy?"

Jack held up a box. "I got some while you were eating lunch."

"Saved me again. I guess this means I have to keep you around for another month or two." He settled back into the seat and took Catherine's hand. The electricity she'd felt when they'd touched that first time he'd come into her office was there again, this time even stronger. She wasn't sure if she was more unnerved by that or by how much she enjoyed it.

"So, I'm a ruthless businessman, a player when it comes to women ... what else do you hold against me?"

She had no intention of telling him she held the same thing against him she did every other man outside her family—she didn't know if she could trust him not to hurt her. So she changed the subject to something more impersonal. "You got the Bonny Blue branding campaign I wanted."

He threw his head back and laughed so loudly, he startled Jack who jerked the steering wheel to the right, almost sending the Escalade onto the shoulder of the road.

"Jeez, Dominic. Warn me before you bellow again, will you? I could have killed us all."

"Sorry, Jack. Catherine's being very amusing back here."

"More like giving you a run for your money."

"Which is a good thing, is it?"

"Absolutely. You need someone other than me to keep you in line. She's a pro at it after only one outing. I'd say that makes her a keeper."

"I agree." Dominic was grinning at her by now. "But I'm not sure she's interested."

"Then work harder at it. She's worth it."

"You both know I'm still here and completely conscious, don't you?" Catherine asked to end the embarrassing turn the conversation had taken.

Dominic brought her hand to his mouth and kissed the tips of her fingers, one at a time. When he got to her pinky finger, he sucked lightly on it, sending an unexpected jolt of desire along nerve bundles that hadn't been stimulated for some time.

"I absolutely know you're here, *cara*. And forgive me. Jack and I have been riding around cooped up in this hunk of metal trash-talking each other for so long, we've forgotten how to behave when someone else is with us. You apologize to the lady, too, Jack."

"I'm sorry, Ms. Bennett, if you were offended."

"Catherine, please. And I was more embarrassed than offended. But thank you, Jack."

"Let's get back to the conversation we were having before Jack so rudely interrupted. The Bonny Blue account—there's nothing I can do about the fact we got the contract, although I have to say I was pleased with what we did for them, and so were they. It was some of our best work."

"And it won you all sorts of awards, which were, I admit, well deserved."

"So, moving on from the business we weren't going to discuss—the other two things you were annoyed about—my unscrupulous professional practices and my sordid reputation with women—have Sergio and Jack improved my image over the past few hours?"

"I guess I'd have to say yes. Although it's probably all the wine and good food talking." She smiled to take some of the sting of her words away.

"Have I been rehabilitated enough to get you to have dinner with me tomorrow night?"

"My son Noah has a soccer tournament in Villanova tomorrow that's going to go on until who knows when, so I have to say no."

"Soccer? This time of year?" He frowned. "Hiding behind your son is beneath you, don't you think?"

"It's not a mixed metaphor of an excuse, Dominic. It's the truth. He's in a year-round soccer program. For the first time, his team made the playoffs for the summer season."

"My apologies. How about next Friday?"

"I'll think about it." She closed her eyes for a few seconds. "Okay."

"Okay … meaning?"

"Okay, I'll have dinner with you."

"That took an encouragingly short time to consider." He leaned over and took her face in his hands. "But then, I did warn you I'm persuasive."

Even in the air-conditioned car she could feel heat. This time she admitted what she'd known before but didn't want to face— the heat wasn't from the summer weather. It was the feel of him touching her, of being close to her. Her throat was so tight she could barely get a sentence out. "I think … I mean … it was Sergio and Jack who convinced me."

"Perhaps I should do some convincing of my own then." He drew her face closer to his, and his lips touched hers, gently at first, so she thought it would be a sweet, almost innocent kiss. She should have known better. Just at the point she thought he might end the kiss, the tip of his tongue began to tease her lips, asking for her to let him in, to let him taste her. Her brain told her to resist, not to give in until she knew if he was safe to trust. Her body said something different. She wanted this, had wanted it ever since he'd kissed her fingers. Maybe even before.

She sighed and her lips parted, letting his tongue slide over hers and giving him access so he could explore her mouth. He tasted of wine and something she couldn't define. Something hot and exciting, something simply Dominic. He didn't devour her, he sampled, as if she were the most delicious of delicacies. Somehow it made her want him more than if he had been aggressive. She was about to wrap her arms around his neck when Jack coughed. Dominic pulled away from the kiss and looked toward the front seat.

"We're almost at the building, Dominic. I thought you'd like to know."

"Thanks, Jack." He rubbed his thumb over her mouth as if to seal in the kiss. "It's back to work I'm afraid, Catherine."

"Right. Work." She pulled her face away from him and pushed herself back into the corner of the seat. "Thank you very much for lunch, Dominic. It was an unexpected treat."

She could swear he was having difficulty keeping a straight face. It almost made her annoyed. Actually, she would have laughed, too, if he had suddenly gone all prim and proper on her, as she'd done.

"You're most welcome. It was my pleasure. We'll do it again." He frowned slightly. "If you're going to Villanova tomorrow, will you still be in the office in the morning?"

"Early. About seven, so I can get in a couple hours of work before the game. Saturdays are about the only time I have any quiet so I can get some writing done."

"Can I bring you coffee to help you think?"

"You don't have to …"

"I know I don't, but I want to. I'll see you about eight."

The Escalade stopped in front of their building; Jack killed the engine and hopped out to open the curbside door for them.

"It was nice meeting you, Catherine," he said as she slid out. He handed her the box of saltwater taffy. "I'm sure I'll be seeing you again."

Chapter 6

"So, did you have a nice time?" Mel asked, the expression on her face verging on a leer as she trailed Catherine down the hall to her office. "I hear the restaurant where you ate is good."

Was it too much to ask that Melody be someplace else? Couldn't she have left early or been out on an errand? No, of course not. Here she was, waiting like a spider for her prey.

"How would you know about the restaurant? Oh, right, your new BFF told you when he called you behind my back." Catherine shoved the box of candy into her friend's hand. "Here's your thirty pieces of silver. I didn't know you could be bought for such a measly price."

Melody looked hurt. "I didn't betray you. All I did was agree you should take an afternoon off and have a nice lunch. Besides, I was looking forward to living vicariously when you came back and told me all the good stuff. Like what is was like to kiss him."

"Why do you think I'd know that?" Catherine busied herself with the papers on her desk, avoiding Melody's gaze. "We just had lunch."

"Sure, lunch explains your flushed face."

"It's hot out."

"Your shiny eyes."

"We drank wine at lunch."

"Your smeared lipstick."

"Oh, hell …" Catherine's hand flew to her mouth. "Wait. I didn't have any lipstick on."

The leer reappeared. "So, to go back to my original question— what's it like to kiss him?"

Catherine marched across her office and snatched the box of taffy from Melody. "You don't deserve this. Not only did you rat me out to Mister … to Dominic but now you're playing games with me."

"You almost said it, didn't you? Mister Sex on Legs. Please tell me he's as hot as he looks."

Catherine struggled to keep a straight face but finally gave in and smiled. "He's smart and charming and funny and …"

"The hell with *charming and funny*. Get to the good stuff."

"He kissed me goodbye, I guess you can say, a couple blocks before we got to the building. It was … nice."

"Don't disappoint me. I can't believe it was *nice*."

"Okay, better than nice. It was … well … apparently my face is flushed and my eyes are shiny." She shrugged, as if to say *figure it out yourself.*

"All my little fantasies about him are true, aren't they?" Melody clapped her hands like a nursery school child and did a little happy dance. "I'm so excited! Now I'll know someone who's part of the hot gossip instead of just hearing about strangers." Suddenly Melody stopped her dance and stared at Catherine, the smile gone. "Wait. That look on your face. I've never seen it before. You're not thinking this will turn into something serious, are you? Please tell me you're not."

"No, of course not. It was just lunch, like the note with the flowers said."

She must not have sounded convincing because Melody continued. "Don't get your hopes up for anything more than that. He's Mister Sex on Legs all right—for half the women in the city. He's been the most eligible bachelor in Philly two—"

"Three."

"Three? Three times?" Mel looked more confused than irritated at having her warning interrupted. "I thought you didn't know much about him outside business."

"He told me."

"There you are, then. He brags about being known for being unattached."

"No, it wasn't like that. He corrected me when I said it had been a couple times."

"Okay, fine, you brought it up. But he made sure you knew the correct number." She put her arm around her friend. "Look, Catherine, I've been telling you for months, maybe even years, you need to look at men as something other than the suits we do business with. But are you sure he's what you're looking for? I don't think there's long-term potential there."

"How do you know what I'm looking for? Maybe I don't want long term. Let me correct that—I *know* I don't want long term. I'm not ready for that yet. But something to jumpstart my clinically dead social life? That I think I am ready for. Finally. If I can get over my reservations about why he's paying attention to me, who would be better for a fling than the man even you think is the sexiest man in the city."

Melody squinted her eyes and stared. "I can't tell whether or not you're serious. Which is not a good sign because I usually can." She sighed. "All right. Have it your way. Besides, if you're only having a fling, you might be more willing to share details like how he kisses or how good he is in bed. It's sad, but at the moment I have to live through you."

"What happened to lunch with the hot guy?"

"Turns out he's hot for the other team. I can't read you, and my gaydar's off. Not a good day." She paused before adding, "Don't get in too deep with Dominic, Catherine. If he hurts you, I'll have to kill him, and then I'll end up in prison. I don't think I'd like the food there."

"I'm sorry about your lunch, and I appreciate the support. But there won't be any need for felony murder, I'm sure." She picked up a pile of papers and sorted through them without seeing what was on the pages. "Now get out of my office and let me try to get some order in here." She indicated the stacks of paper and sample publications scattered about the room.

Melody grabbed her box of candy then asked one more question as she headed for the door. "Are you seeing him again?"

Catherine hesitated for a few seconds but finally gave in with a small smile. "Coffee tomorrow and dinner next Friday."

"Who knew this would happen when we moved into the building?"

Melody closed the door, leaving Catherine standing in the middle of the evidence of a chaotic week, touching her mouth with her fingertips and saying softly, "Yeah, who knew?"

• • •

Dominic arrived in time to get coffee for himself and Catherine and get to her office by eight, as he'd promised. He'd considered being at her office door when she arrived at seven but thought that might be a bit too eager. And he didn't do eager. However, he was surprised at how much he was looking forward to seeing her again. Somehow, on the strength of an extended elevator flirtation, one lunch, and a kiss that seemed to promise there might be more to come, he had begun to anticipate their time together in ways not usual for him.

The door to her office suite was open although no one was at the front desk. He could hear voices coming from down the hall but decided not to wait for someone to acknowledge his presence. He knew where her office was, after all. But when he knocked on the closed door, he got no response. He tried again. Still nothing. She was either someplace else or completely wrapped up in her work.

Betting on the latter, he opened the door and said, "Delivery for Bennett." She looked up from her computer with a startled expression.

"Oh, God, is it eight already?" she asked.

"It's nice to see you, too, Catherine," he said.

"Let me start over. Good morning, Dominic. How lovely of you to bring me coffee."

"That's better." Plucking one cup from the carrier, he handed it to her with a flourish. "A double-shot, skinny latte for the lady."

"It is altogether too stalker-ish that you not only know my credit history, my maiden name, and who-knows-what-else about me, but you also know how I drink my coffee."

"I don't. Didn't. But the barista downstairs does." He moved the visitor's chair closer to her desk before making himself comfortable. "You didn't say what you were working on today that brought you in so early. Big project?"

"Yeah. I need to get this draft edited for my project manager before I leave. What're you doing?"

"My usual Saturday drill. Going over the billings and financials."

"I thought you had a CFO."

"I do, but I like to know what's going on, so I look at the weekly report he leaves me every Friday."

"I'm not crazy about that part of my job, but I can't rationalize taking on a CFO or a managing partner yet. Not sure I want to." She took a long drink of her coffee. "I know I said I didn't want to talk business with you but I'm curious—you're the managing director and Edie's the creative director, right?"

"Correct. I split the responsibilities about five years ago. We'd gotten big enough it was hard for me to keep track of everything by myself."

"How can you confine yourself only to the business side of the firm? Don't you miss the creative side of your work? I would."

"Edie may be creative director, but I have a hand in every piece of work, every image, every word that goes out the door. It's my name on that door, after all. So I don't miss the creative side. I still do some of it."

"I can only hope someday I have someone working here who loves the business side as much as I love the creative side. Until then …" She let the sentence drift off.

"You'll get there."

She gestured to her computer. "If I have enough of these projects, maybe I will."

"Sounds like I should let you get back to work." He rose from the chair.

Walking him to the door, she said, "Thank you again for the coffee. I need all the caffeine I can get today."

"It was only an excuse to see you again. You do know that, don't you?"

She didn't say anything, merely looked up into his brown eyes and smiled.

"You have beautiful eyes," he said as he traced around them with his forefinger. "And wonderful cheekbones. Then there's this mouth. I've thought about it a lot since yesterday." He trailed his finger over her cheek and then to her top lip. "What I realized was, I didn't taste it nearly enough yesterday. I'd like to correct that omission."

He didn't want to rush her, but he needed to kiss her again, needed to feel her mouth against his. He started softly, sweetly, not knowing how far she would want him to push. But her lips parted without any urging from him, and when her body relaxed against him, he responded with a swift exploration of her mouth with the tip of his tongue. She tasted of coffee and the same sweetness he'd discovered when he'd kissed her in his SUV. She sighed into his mouth and her arms went around him.

He pulled her closer and shifted his mouth to make it possible to nibble on her lower lip, then, taking his time, he deepened the kiss. The temptation to keep going, to find out what her skin felt like under the T-shirt she wore, was strong. Maybe even to see how comfortable that little couch of hers was with the two of them horizontal on it.

But he knew he couldn't push that far that fast. So he nipped at her lip again then kissed where he had nipped before drawing back from her. She frowned slightly, as if disappointed the kiss was over. Smiling, he dropped a kiss on her forehead and said, "If I don't go now, I'm quite likely to do something that will seriously interfere with either of us getting any more work done."

"Yes. I guess we should both get back to … to … whatever." She didn't move away from him, however, but continued to look up at him, her eyes wide and unfocused. He wanted to kiss her again, to make sure when she went back to work she wouldn't forget who had made her feel that way. But before he had a chance to act on his impulse, the door to the office flew open and whacked him in the back.

Melody barged in. "Catherine, you haven't answered the email I sent about the links to the research you were—" When she saw who was standing there, the doorknob still in the small of his back, she stopped talking and flushed a deep red. "Oh, Mr. Russo. I thought Catherine was alone. I'm so, so sorry. Maybe I should come back later."

"No harm, no foul, Melody. And it's Dominic." He smiled at the obviously rattled woman. "I brought Catherine coffee, but I was just leaving."

"Coffee—right. Don't forget yours," Catherine said. She grabbed his cup from her desk and handed it to him. "Thanks again for the latte."

"Any time." He was almost out the door when he thought to add, "I hope Noah has a good tournament today."

"Thanks. I have my fingers crossed for him."

• • •

The silence left by Dominic's departure went on for several moments. Finally Catherine said, "There was a reason you barged in, I assume."

Melody shook herself out of her stunned speechlessness. "Oh, right. Sorry. I wanted to make sure you checked your email. I came in this morning to finish up the research you wanted for the Butterfly Trust proposal. My laptop died and I needed a computer. Check what I sent you, please, and make sure it's what you need. I'm nervous about my first research assignment from you." She ducked her head in apology. "I'm sorry I interrupted you and Mister Sex on Legs. He was about to kiss you, wasn't he?"

Before she answered, Catherine returned to her desk and began to pull up the message Melody mentioned. "Got it. I'll take a look before I leave."

"You didn't answer my question. I barged in just when he was going to kiss you, didn't I?"

"No, as a matter of fact, you didn't. He wasn't."

"I'm sure he was. I could see it on his face."

"Trust me, he wasn't about to kiss me." Catherine was sure her smug smile would give her away.

It did. "Oh. Now I see. He wasn't *about* to kiss you. He already had. Although from the look on his face, he was thinking about doing it again." She frowned and pursed her lips before adding, "I thought you said you still had reservations."

"Maybe I decided not to be wary of a perfectly nice man who's shown some interest in me."

"You went from scared silly to sex in the office in one day? Wow. Yay, team Bennett! Pompoms waving. Way to go."

"Melody, don't let this run away with you. There was no sex in the office. Only a little kiss."

"Right. So the sex will be on Friday when you have dinner with him."

"No, it won't. Noah's there, remember? And I thought you said it was a bad idea for me to get involved with a man like Dominic."

"Yeah, but I've changed my mind. You convinced me. If you want to have a fling, who better to have it with than an expert?

One of us needs to see what all the gossip is about." She had her hand on the doorknob when she added, "But you better not fall for him."

Chapter 7

Driving to Villanova took longer than Catherine expected. Or more accurately, *seemed* to take longer, it was so uncomfortable.

The discomfort started when, ten minutes into the trip, Noah asked, "Is something wrong, Mom?"

"Not really." Catherine had been quiet, trying to decide if now was the best time to tell Noah about Dominic—who he'd meet on Friday. On one hand, she couldn't look him in the eye while she was driving to see how he was taking the news. On the other, Noah was stuck in the car and couldn't storm out the way he sometimes did when he didn't like what she was saying. "Does it seem like there is?"

"I don't know. Maybe. You aren't talking much. You haven't even asked what I was up to while you were at work, and you always do."

"I'm sorry. I've been thinking about something. Actually, trying to think of a way to talk to you about something."

"Not another sex talk. Please. You and Dad covered that years ago."

She didn't have to see his face to know he was rolling his eyes. "It's not about you. And it's not about sex. Well, not specifically. It's about dating."

"I'm not dating. Nobody dates anymore. Except old people. I guess they still have dates."

"Still not about you." *Here goes.* "I had a lunch date yesterday."

"With a man?"

He sounded surprised, skeptical even. If she needed proof she'd been living a socially sheltered life, the tone of his voice gave it to her. "Yes, with a man. We had lunch yesterday, and we're going to dinner next Friday."

Noah was quiet for what seemed like a long time. Catherine waited for him to continue the conversation. "What about Dad?"

"What about him? We're divorced."

"Yeah, but you could still get back together someday, and how're you gonna do that if you're hooking up with some guy?"

"First of all, I'm not 'hooking up' with anyone. Second, he's not 'some guy.' His name is Dominic Russo; he's a nice man; he owns the building where my new office is. Third …"

"Oh, great. He's Italian. Nonna will be happy. Is that why you're doing this? So she won't be mad at you forever about getting a divorce?"

"Would you please let me finish responding to one outrageous statement before you make another? You know your dad and I aren't getting back together. For heaven's sake, Noah, even if I wanted to get back with him—and I don't—his being married doesn't bode well for reconciliation, do you think?"

"But suppose he leaves Susan and you're with this Russo guy?"

Catherine took a couple deep breaths, trying to keep herself from pounding on the steering wheel. Which was only a replacement for wanting to find a way to pound the simple fact into her son's head that, no matter what he wanted, she and his dad were never going to be a couple again because neither of them *wanted* to be a couple again.

"Noah, I thought you'd gotten over this idea that your dad's coming back. He's not. We've moved on with our lives. For me, right now, it means I'm having dinner with Dominic this Friday. And for your information, I'm not now, nor have I ever, gone to dinner with anyone to please your grandmother."

If she hadn't remembered only too clearly how she'd tormented her mother when she was a teenager, she'd have been royally pissed off at her son for his attitude. She needed to talk to her ex—again—and make sure he knew Noah was still pining for his parents to reconcile.

"Can I meet this guy? Or are you going to go out with him secretly?"

"Secretly? When I'm telling you about him? You'll meet him when he comes to pick me up on Friday. And I expect you to be polite. You may get away with snark when you talk to me, but he doesn't deserve it."

The rest of the drive was in a silence broken only by the sound of the music Noah chose to play from his iPod which, unfortunately, was both more raucous than she liked and connected to the car's speakers. She let him get away with it because she wasn't up for another fight.

The first game went well for Noah's team, although he seemed a little slow getting into the rhythm of the game. His team won and went on to the semifinal round, but Noah continued to play with less focus than usual. Eventually his coach replaced him with a younger team member. They lost when the opposing team scored a last-minute goal, and Noah's team was out of the series. Catherine was relieved she wouldn't be driving to some suburb or another the next weekend for the finals, but she knew the team would be disappointed, even though the semifinal round was further than they had ever gotten before.

Catherine stayed on the sideline while the requisite after-game team handshakes and snacking took place. When Noah separated from his teammates and began to clomp toward her, she folded up her chair and waited for him to join her. She winced at the expression on his face, the worst case of teenage sulk she'd seen in a long time, and knew the ride home wasn't going to be any better than the ride there had been.

He didn't stop when he reached her but continued stomping his way to the car. She had to take long strides to keep up. "You guys did great. The first game may have been the best I've seen you play all season."

"We should have won the second game, too. We only lost it because you made me lose focus and I got pulled. The kid Coach put in didn't have the experience to keep the other team from getting that last goal."

"*I* made you lose focus? How?"

"I couldn't concentrate because of the stuff you told me in the car about this guy you're suddenly dating." They'd reached her CRV, and Noah yanked on the back hatch, which was locked. Catherine pushed the button on the remote to open it, but as she did, Noah pulled at the latch again. She zapped and he yanked at the same time a second time. After the third unsuccessful try, she asked him to step away from the back of the car so she could get it open. He threw her a black look but complied. This time when she zapped, the hatch opened.

Noah threw his cleats and team sweatshirt into the back. Catherine loaded her chair. They got into the car for the long, silent drive home.

• • •

Catherine was beginning to believe Dominic came in at the same time she did every morning on purpose. It was too coincidental that she ran into him in the lobby of the building almost every day, or that he walked into the coffee bar as she was ordering her latte before going up to her office.

On this particular Monday, she crossed paths with him in the coffee shop. His smile was as warm as the temperature outside and much more welcome.

"How'd Noah's team do in the tournament?" he asked.

"They aced the first game and came close to winning their semifinal round. Lost by one goal in the last minute."

"Noah must have been disappointed."

"Disappointed and angry at me."

"You? What did you do? Flirt with the coach so he was too distracted to do his job? You could certainly distract me."

Catherine tsked her displeasure, making his smile even bigger.

He touched her elbow, directing her to a table. "I have ten minutes to hear this story. Do you have ten to tell me?"

She nodded, deciding she might as well prepare him now for what was going to happen on Friday. "I guess so. Particularly since it involves you, too."

"To the best of my knowledge I've never been responsible for a soccer team losing a game. Come to think of it, I've never flirted with a soccer coach either."

"And neither have I." She played with the sleeve on the cup, trying to sort out what she wanted to say. "On the way to the game, I told Noah I'd had a lunch date on Friday and would have a dinner date this Friday. He was not amused and implied I was cheating on his father."

"I'm curious how one cheats on an ex-spouse."

"It seems Noah still thinks there's a chance his dad and I will get back together. And if I'm having dinner with 'some guy,' as he put it, it's being untrue to his fantasy."

"It's not uncommon with kids, is it, to want their parents back together?"

"No, but we've had this conversation dozens of times. Both his father and I have told him it's not going to happen. I don't want it, and his father's wife might find it inconvenient at the very least. I thought it was a moot point."

"How's he dealt with the other men you've been out with?"

There was an uncomfortable silence. "Well, that's probably part of the problem. I haven't been out with anyone since the divorce."

"I know you said you didn't really have much of a social life, but it's hard to believe there's been no one at all."

"There hasn't been. Not unless you count women friends, sisters, and a son."

This time the silence came from Dominic's side of the table, as he seemed to be digesting what he'd heard. He shook his head. "What's wrong with all the men you've met? I assumed you had them standing in line waiting to ask you out."

"It's not them, it's me."

He shuddered. "Please. Not that line. It's too reminiscent of a bad breakup."

"Did you hear it or use it?" She couldn't help laughing at his attempt to lighten the conversation.

"Sadly, heard it. Never used it, never will." He touched her hand. "But explain to me why you've turned down chances to have a social life."

"I had a son to raise and a business to grow. Which took all the energy I had. Besides, there hasn't been anyone interested. Even if there had been, it wouldn't have made a difference."

He cocked his head and frowned. "I'm not sure I should ask this, but I will. Why did you say yes to me, then? And no excuses about how I was threatening to endanger a plant species."

She hesitated but decided there was no point in avoiding the answer. He deserved the truth. "Moving into this building made me feel I was making a success of my business. And things were good with Noah. It seemed like it was time to do something just for me."

"And there I was?"

"Well, there was a bit more to it. I was flattered that someone like … that you'd pay attention to me. You made me think about things I hadn't considered in years, had even forgotten I liked."

"Lucky me." His expression said he wasn't being clever or sarcastic. The warm look in his eyes said he meant it.

"You may change your mind after you meet Noah on Friday."

"I'm forty-five. Thirteen-year-old boys don't have enough experience to make a dent in my self-esteem. And anyway, I was an adolescent male once. I know how they operate."

"Then maybe sometime you'll explain it to me."

Dominic glanced at his watch then finished his coffee. "I'd be happy to, but I don't have time right now." He stood and pitched his cup into a waste bin. "Maybe we could start at lunch on Wednesday. You free?"

"Depends on where you want to eat. I have client meetings all Wednesday afternoon, so revisiting Sergio is out of the question."

"I was thinking more of a place a couple blocks away—Thai Noodles."

"I love that place. I usually have to settle for takeout, though. Going there would be a treat. Is twelve thirty okay?" She picked up her cup and walked with him to the elevator. "But you don't have to keep feeding me, you know."

"I'm Italian. It's what we do. You should know that. And twelve thirty works."

•••

Dominic was puzzled. Catherine was beautiful and smart, successful, and available. She should be beating men off with a stick. Was there more to her dateless state than simply wanting to focus on her business and her son? From the few comments she made about her husband, he had to wonder if she had a bad case of "once burned, twice shy." He understood how it could happen. His own brief marriage—which he usually referred to as twenty minutes of his life he'd never get back—had soured him on serious relationships from his early twenties, when the marriage had begun and ended, well into his thirties, when another relationship had cemented the habit of avoiding emotional entanglements. But he hadn't closed himself off from enjoying the opposite sex and what they offered him. Catherine apparently had.

Had he known what she'd revealed, would he have changed the way he'd approached her? No, probably not. What he'd done had gotten him lunch, coffee, another lunch, and dinner—all in one week. Throw in a couple kisses he replayed every now and then because they'd been so pleasurable, and it had all worked out fine.

Still, knowing what he now knew would make a change in what he did next. He didn't have a timeline for taking a woman to bed, but he was willing to bet Catherine wouldn't meet it if he had one. Which was too bad. Kissing her had not only given him interesting moments to contemplate, but had also whetted his appetite for more. She was delicious, so aroused when they kissed, with her brown eyes going black and her lovely skin flushing with desire.

But he knew she would likely take her time before going any further. He had to find a way to make her comfortable, let her know, no matter how much he wanted her, he was willing to wait until she was ready.

He'd work on it at lunch.

Chapter 8

Thai iced tea had been served, and pad Thai and crispy fried noodles ordered. Dominic was about to launch into his speech about not wanting her to feel he was putting pressure on her when she said, "So, what's it like to be a thirteen-year-old male?"

He was surprised. "You were serious?"

"This is my chance to try and understand this strange creature I'm living with, and I'm not passing it up. Didn't you mean what you said?"

"I was mostly joking, but if you're really interested …" A memory of another conversation tickled the edge of his mind. "Didn't you say you have a brother? Don't you remember what he was like as a teenager?"

"He's three years younger than I am. I don't remember much about his teenage years except I had a few friends who wanted to hang out at my house because they thought he was cute. I didn't understand it because, to me, he was too young to pay attention to." She shrugged her shoulders. "Besides, sometimes I think Tony—my brother—is part of Noah's attitude issues. After his father moved out, Noah got even closer to his uncle. Then Tony got married and moved to the Northwest. Two men he loved. Two men who left."

"Does Noah see his dad regularly?"

"Not really. Andy, my ex, doesn't operate that way. He's not a bad father. He loves Noah, and we work okay together as parents. He isn't a regularly scheduled father, I guess you can say. Noah doesn't see him more than once or twice a month. In a way, Tony's been more attentive. He talks to Noah every week, has flown him out to Oregon once already, and is making noises about having him come out between Christmas and New Year's."

"Losing both of them sounds like it might have been rough on Noah. No wonder you're asking perfect strangers for advice."

"You're hardly a stranger. And I have yet to be convinced you're perfect. So, get to what you were like when you were thirteen."

He lounged back in his seat and shrugged. "Okay, if you're really interested. It's not a completely pretty story. And you have to remember, when I was thirteen Ben Franklin was flying a kite around here someplace. Things might be different now."

"I'm desperate here, Russo. I'll take any help I can get."

"Well, what I remember was feeling unsure about what was happening to me. My body was changing; my head was full of ideas I didn't know how to handle. I was angry about not understanding it. All I wanted to do was beat up on something."

"You got in fights?" Incredulousness was evident in the tone of her voice.

"Constantly. My younger brother was the athlete in the family, so he wore himself out with basketball and track. I was never much interested in team sports, so I got into fights."

"About?"

"Girls. Imagined slights. Sometimes nothing at all. It was a way to let off steam. I spent the better part of my early teen years with banged-up knuckles, cuts on my face, and the occasional black eye. Noah's lucky he has soccer. It's a much more productive way to use up energy."

"Sounds like *I'm* lucky he has soccer."

"You're undoubtedly right."

The waiter interrupted with their lunch. They both attacked their noodles and let the conversation lag for a few minutes.

Eventually Catherine continued, "I assumed middle school is the same stew of hormones for boys as it is for girls, but I didn't think about the difference in how they'd act. I don't think I knew any girls who got into fights. Lots of mean-girl stuff, but not physical fights."

Dominic sat up straight as Catherine's words jogged a memory. "Middle school girls. My God. I haven't thought about Cathy Evans in years."

"Your middle school girlfriend?"

"Yeah. In seventh grade, we got caught making out in the janitor's closet. Our parents were brought in to the principal's office to discuss our 'inappropriate behavior.'"

Catherine giggled.

"It wasn't funny at the time. We got detention for a couple weeks."

"Dragging a girl into a closet to kiss her doesn't quite go with the image I have of the very smooth and sophisticated Dominic Russo."

"There was no dragging involved, believe me, but I'm relieved you're not worried I'll repeat that particular approach to male-female relationships."

She raised an eyebrow at him. "You came dangerously close with the lunch at the shore stunt, but I've decided to let it pass. How did your parents deal with it?"

"Interesting reaction. I overheard my father say in a conversation I was clearly not supposed to hear that kissing a girl when you were thirteen wasn't inappropriate behavior at all, it was normal."

"And your mother?"

"She was more in your camp—outraged I'd taken the girl to a janitor's closet. She said she thought she'd raised me with more class. But in spite of their belief what I'd done wasn't all that bad, they backed the school. They told me I had to learn to respect the rules even if I didn't agree with them. To work to change the rules, not disobey them. And they took me to task for getting someone else in trouble with my behavior—although, technically, it was *our* behavior."

"How'd they deal with the fighting?"

"They were even harder on me. When the school threatened to expel me if I got in one more fight, I was grounded for a whole semester. Had to earn my way back into being trusted by doing all sorts of good deeds."

"I think I like their parenting style. I might steal some of those ideas. And you've made me feel more comfortable about you and Noah meeting on Friday. You really do understand the species." She looked at the time on her phone. "I better be getting back. A new client's coming in for our first meeting at two, and I want to go over the presentation with the project manager."

"Can you give me about five more minutes?"

"We can finish the conversation about male puberty on Friday, can't we?"

"About Friday—I want to say something so we're both clear what's happening." He slid closer to her in the booth and took her hand. "I've been thinking about what you said the other morning, about not having a … shall we say … social life for the last three years."

She sighed and broke eye contact. "If you've decided I'm too rusty at the kind of extracurricular life you usually have, I understand. We don't have to have dinner on—"

"You really do have some interesting ideas of who I am, don't you? First I was a ruthless businessman, then a low-life player. A few minutes ago I was so smooth and sophisticated I'd never drag a girl into a janitor's closet for a kiss. Now I'm apparently willing to ditch the woman I've been trying to go out with for weeks because she's had the good sense not waste her time with other men before she met me."

"I guess what I wanted to say didn't come out right. I only meant …"

"You meant it was okay for me to break our date if I'd changed my mind when I found out you'd been out of the game since your divorce." Now it was his turn to sigh—in frustration. "Is it because you think all I want is to get you into bed, or is there some other reason?"

She pulled her hand out from under his and started playing with the chopsticks, moving the leftover noodles around on her plate, not meeting his gaze, a pink flush on her cheeks. "I thought I was letting you off the hook. You looked so surprised that morning."

"I was. For the reason I gave you. I'd have thought men would be beating down your door to take you out. And I don't buy the comment no one has been interested." He chewed on his lip for a minute. "Tell me something. When the roses started arriving, who did you think was sending them?"

She looked startled at the question then hesitated for a few moments before answering. "I wasn't sure, but my staff had a betting pool on who it was. There were a few weird candidates like the barista downstairs, but the three main contenders were a freelance copy editor I hire frequently, a former client, and ..." She stopped.

"And me, right?"

"Well, yes. And you."

"So apparently your staff noticed three men who'd shown interest in you. Right?"

"I guess."

"You haven't been ignored, Catherine. You've ignored anyone who's interested. Your staff knows it. I know it. But for some reason, you don't want to see it. Hell, it cost me a fortune to get your attention. And, for the record, it's not just for a tumble into my bed. Although if you'd like that, I'm perfectly willing to oblige you."

"Dominic, this is bordering on embarrassing."

"I'm simply trying to say it's been obvious to half my staff and, apparently, a good proportion of yours, that I find you attractive. And from the way you kiss me, you feel the same about me. I'm not going to break our dinner date because I've discovered you've buried yourself in work and in raising your son for the last three years."

He kissed her hand. "I have every intention of being with you in a restaurant on Friday night so we can continue to have these interesting talks about what kind of dastardly—wasn't that the word you used?—egomaniac I am."

"Now we've made it into downtown embarrassing."

"Then I have nothing to lose by saying this: I want you. I've wanted you since the day I first saw you. But I'm in no hurry. And I won't put pressure on you."

"I'm not sure what to say."

"Say you're still interested in having dinner with me on Friday. And you agree to let this attraction between us develop along its natural course."

"Dinner, I'm fine with. But for the other—I'm so out of practice, I have no idea how to go about it."

After thinking about what she said for a moment or two, he replied, "Pick a code word."

"A code word? For what?" She seemed both curious and baffled.

"Some word you can say to me when you decide you're ready to take the next step."

"Like a reverse safe word?"

He pursed his mouth and frowned. "What the hell do you know about safe words?"

"I may have been off the market for a while, but I read widely." She was positively indignant.

"Okay, yes, like a reverse safe word. What do you think?"

"Well, it'll have to be a word I wouldn't ordinarily use. And I think it should be Italian."

"I meant what do you think about the idea, but I agree, it would have to be a word we wouldn't use in normal conversation. But why Italian?"

"It seems … appropriate, I guess. It might take me a while, though, to think of a word. Sadly, I never learned the language. Except for swearing. I'm good at swearing in several languages, Italian included. But I use those words. So I'll have to think of something else."

Dominic signaled for the check, and after he let her win the argument to split it, they paid and left.

They were back in their office building when Catherine abruptly turned to him and said, "Tiramisu."

What did a dessert have to do with anything they'd been discussing? "Pardon?"

"The code word. Tiramisu."

"Okay. It's not what I would have predicted, but it'll work. Why'd you pick it?"

"It's Italian. It's not something I say every day. And it's in one of my favorite movie scenes. In *Sleepless in Seattle*, Tom Hanks's friend lets him think tiramisu is a new sex move."

People turned around in the lobby to see what was so funny as Dominic let loose with a belly laugh. "Maybe tiramisu isn't as inappropriate as I thought it was. But this means Italian restaurants are definitely out for a while."

Chapter 9

"I'll get it, Mom," Noah yelled from the kitchen.

Catherine had heard the doorbell, too, and was already in the entryway. "I'm here. It's Dominic, I imagine." She could hear the snort from two rooms away. Although she'd been preparing for this all day—hell, all week—she was nervous about how it would play out.

"No roses; I remembered," Dominic said after he kissed her on the forehead. He handed her a bud vase with several sprays of small, delicate dendrobium orchids in it.

She gave him the smile she knew he was aiming for. "They're beautiful. Thank you." Catherine carried the vase into the living room and put it on the table in front of the love seat. "I really did enjoy the roses. Sort of. Although I hear your staff enjoyed them more."

He followed her. "They did. They enjoyed them so much, I may consider doing it again in place of bonuses."

"I wasn't so lucky. Melody almost led an angry mob up to your floor to retrieve some of them when she heard I'd left the whole cart full in your office." She saw Noah standing in the door of the living room. "Come, join us," she said, motioning to him. Noah didn't budge.

"Hi," Dominic said, extending his hand and taking a few steps toward her son. "You must be Noah. I'm Dominic Russo."

"Yeah, I figured."

To Catherine's embarrassment, Noah didn't shake hands. She spoke quickly to cover his rudeness. "We're about to leave, Noah. Your dinner's in the oven. If you go to Rudy's house afterward, text me so I know, please."

"You going to some Italian place for dinner?" he asked, directing the question to his mother, not Dominic.

Catherine tried not to look at her date, but she couldn't ignore him when she heard his stifled laugh. She giggled.

"What's so funny?" Noah asked. "It's not a hard question."

"Private joke, Noah. Sorry, didn't mean to be rude," Dominic said. "We're going to a French restaurant downtown."

"The French eat snails and frog legs," Noah said. "Who'd eat that?"

"Me. I like snails and frog legs." Catherine put her arm around her pouting son and kissed his cheek. He predictably pulled away. "I'll be home in a few hours," she said.

"It doesn't take a few hours to eat dinner." He finally looked at Dominic. "What else do you have planned for tonight? Or are you just going to spring it on her?"

Softly, but with a serious tone to his voice, Dominic responded. "Noah, you don't know much about me yet, but let's establish one thing. I have enormous respect for your mother, and I assume you do, too. So I'm going to suggest—I'm going to insist—we not talk like that about or around her."

Noah stormed off in the direction of the steps to the second floor.

Catherine closed her eyes and wondered if she'd made a mistake trying to have a personal life before her son went to college. Or to juvenile detention. Whichever came first.

• • •

After the rocky start, the evening with Dominic had nowhere to go but up. And it definitely did. Dinner was delicious, the company wonderful. But then, Catherine was only too aware how good every hour she spent with him was. Gradually, with his attention and his sense of humor, not to mention the way his kisses made her feel, he was chipping away at her reluctance to have more than a simple, safe, lobby-and-elevator relationship with him, For the first time since her husband had left her, she was beginning to wonder if she could trust a man—this man—with her feelings. Her biggest worry now seemed to be how he related to Noah. From Dominic's side, it had gone okay, although she still had work to do with her son.

Maybe after Noah got accustomed to seeing her dating, he'd be better about it. Until then, she could feel relieved Dominic had taken in stride her son's attempts to insult him. At least, he still seemed interested in her. He'd asked her to go with him to the black tie benefit for Opera Philadelphia in mid-September. It was a performance of *Aida*, starring a rising, young, Italian tenor. She'd actually toyed with the idea of buying a ticket and going solo before she'd discovered it was sold-out, so she enthusiastically accepted.

On the strength of that invitation, she asked him to have dinner at her house the following weekend. And in the course of their conversation in the restaurant, they discovered they were both intrigued by the same movie and made a tentative date to see it. Their relationship was coming out of the elevator big time.

As they waited for Jack to pick them up at the restaurant, Dominic asked, "How about I take you to one of my favorite places in the city for a walk before I take you home?"

Jack drove them to the sculpture garden in Fairmount Park. The night was clear. The Schuylkill River was calm. The air was pleasant with a hint of the approach of fall. It was the perfect end to the evening. They walked through the garden, their arms around each other, comparing opinions on the pieces of art. Then Dominic stopped in front of The Poet statue. He didn't say anything, merely turned to face her, put one arm around her waist, and, with the other hand, drew her face to his. His mouth touched hers and the world disappeared around her. Nothing existed except the two of them.

Without his insisting, she parted her lips and his tongue responded, warm and gentle. At first. Then the kiss became more demanding as he deepened it, exploring every inch of her mouth. She circled his neck with her arms; he slipped both hands down to her hips, pulling them tight against his. The evidence of his arousal pushed against her. The evidence of her own curled around in her belly.

The kiss went on and on and on. He nibbled on her lips, bathed them with his tongue, took possession of them again. The breath in her lungs seemed to disappear into his, becoming the very air he inhaled. Every inch of her demanded to be part of him as she pressed against him. Her breasts ached for his touch. She longed to feel her hands on his hot skin.

His hands moved to the sides of her breasts, his mouth kissed down her jawline to the pulse at the base of her throat. A pulse she knew was beating as hard and as fast as the wings of a hummingbird. All she could feel was Dominic. All she wanted was Dominic.

If he could make her feel this way with a kiss, what would it feel like to make love with him? And what was she waiting for? She'd told Melody she wanted a fling, and here was a man who could obviously give her one. Maybe she should scream "tiramisu" at the top of her lungs and run for the Escalade and his apartment. She broke from the kiss, he touched his forehead to hers, and she started to say the word. What came out was …

"Catherine! Catherine!"

No, that wasn't right. *She* was Catherine. Had the kiss confused her so much she was calling Dominic by her own name? But that wasn't right either. She hadn't said anything yet.

"Catherine! Dominic!"

They both turned to see Jack running toward them.

"Your phone keeps ringing, Catherine." He handed it to her. "I was worried it might be an emergency."

Chapter 10

"What the hell did you think you were doing?" Catherine asked. She'd barely gotten Noah into the entryway of their home and the door closed behind her before her frustration boiled over. "Don't bother answering—you weren't thinking. If you'd had half a sensible thought in your head, you'd have known walking out of that store with a six-pack of beer under your shirt was not only illegal but stupid."

"Sorry," Noah muttered.

"Sorry doesn't begin to cover it. What were you doing in that neighborhood anyway? I thought you were going to Rudy's. He doesn't live anywhere near there."

"He didn't want to go out. I was with some other guys."

"You mean the guys who ran away when you got caught stealing beer for them?" She had to dig her nails into the palms of her hands to keep from grabbing his shoulders and shaking him, something she'd never done once in his thirteen years. "Damn it, Noah, if the cop hadn't recognized you as Tony's nephew, if he hadn't known to call your Nonna … do you know how upset she is?"

"Nonna only had to get involved because you were too busy with that guy to answer your phone. It took you forever to get to the store." The disdain in Noah's voice cut her to the bone.

"No, I didn't get there sooner because you wouldn't give them the phone number they wanted. They had to call Nonna to track me down. Do you think by doing something stupid, I'll stop seeing Dominic? Is that what's behind this?"

"No matter what I do, you're going to see him again. Because he's more important."

"Than I am" was unspoken but implied.

By this time she was pacing the floor in front of a defiant-looking Noah. "Fortunately, the owner knew Tony when he was a rookie cop, so he isn't going to press charges. Thanks to your uncle's good reputation you got off easy." She stopped in front of him, trying hard to keep her voice controlled and calm. "But just because you got a pass from the police and the storeowner doesn't mean you get one from me." She started pacing again, not sure she could keep her cool when staring directly into the angry and resentful eyes of her son. "You don't even know how fortunate you are."

"Yeah, yeah. I know. I'm the fucking luckiest kid in town."

"Watch your mouth, Noah. The jury in this house is still out on what's to be done about you, and using bad language doesn't help your case. I have to think about it. And I have to talk to Tony. I imagine your uncle will have a few things to say on the subject when I tell him what happened."

"Why do you have to tell everyone in the family?" Noah asked. "Are you trying to look like the perfect mother or just make me look bad?"

Ignoring the insults, she said, "Of course I'm going to tell Tony. If I don't, he might hear it from his buddy and be hurt I hadn't told him first." She stopped, almost dizzy from hyperventilating and pacing.

"For right now, you're grounded. I haven't decided for how long. While I'm home, consider yourself in my custody. When I'm out, since you can't be trusted on your own, I'll arrange for a babysitter. On school breaks, you'll come to work with me."

For the first time since they'd gotten to the house, Noah's sullen defiance was gone, replaced by outrage. "You can't treat me like that. I'm not a baby," he yelled.

"When you do things like you pulled tonight, you are clearly not mature enough to leave home alone."

"I hate you. I want to live with Dad. He's always around when I go visit him. He doesn't go out on dates."

Right. Because he married the woman he was having an affair with when we were married. And it's easy to be around on the one weekend a month he decides it's convenient to see his son. "I called him while the officer was talking to you and the storeowner. Your father agrees with me. You're stuck here twenty-four seven with me and confined to his condo when you're with him. No soccer. No hanging out with your friends. Nothing but school when it starts and something I'll figure out as community service to make up for the trouble you caused."

"No soccer! That's not fair. Fall practice begins next week. The team needs me."

"You should have thought of the team before you pulled the stunt you did tonight. Now, go to your room."

He stomped away, leaving Catherine helplessly wondering, not for the first time, why parents didn't get operating instructions when their kids became teenagers. Or at the very least a warning.

She was about to make a phone call she was not looking forward to when her cell rang.

"I know it's late but I was concerned about you. How'd things go?" Dominic's soothing voice was the best thing she'd heard in the past four hours.

Catherine related the story of what had happened after Jack dropped her off at the scene of the crime.

"I was about to call Tony and tell him what happened before he gets a call from his friend. He'll be furious."

"Maybe he'll be able to get through to Noah."

"I hope so."

She tried to collect her thoughts before she said what might be the hardest thing she'd had to say since she told her mother she was getting a divorce. "It doesn't take a genius to figure out this was triggered by our dinner date tonight. I think we better reconsider going out together for a while."

There was no response at first, then he said, "Doesn't giving up your personal life get him what he wants with his behavior? Do you think that's wise?"

"I need to put my energy here, with him, right now. Anyway, after tonight I don't trust him home alone." She laughed for the first time in hours. "I told him I was going to get a babysitter for him if I went out. I think he's envisioning some teenager not much older than he is, which really insulted him. I actually meant I'd ask my mother to help out. I know I shouldn't feel this way, but I was happy he was pissed about it. It was the only reaction I got from him other than the sullen, pouty look teenagers seem to have perfected."

"They are good at it, aren't they? At least my nieces and nephew are." She waited for him to say more about her embargo on dates. She wanted him to object, to say he couldn't see how it would help, could only see how much it would hurt them. Instead, he said, "Okay, if that's what you want, I understand. Maybe we could do lunch one day."

"I can't even think what my schedule looks like right now, but if I can, sure."

"We can touch base next week and see."

Do lunch? Touch base? What happened to "I've wanted you since the first time I saw you?" If he was this easily scared off, had she been wrong about his interest in her? "Sure. We can talk sometime next week. Oh, and I don't think I thanked you for dinner tonight. It was lovely."

"I'm sorry the evening didn't end better."

"Me, too."

If there was one good thing the unsatisfactory phone call with Dominic did, it distracted her enough to make the phone call to her brother a bit easier. Getting back to worrying about Noah helped her paper over her disappointment that Dominic didn't put up a bigger fight about not seeing her.

Tony was surprisingly calm. "Look, I'm not trying to downplay what he did or suggest you let him off the hook. You shouldn't," he said, "but I can tell you a hell of a lot of kids do stupid things like this once and get straightened out without any further problems."

"You didn't do anything like this," Catherine said. "At least I don't remember you did."

"You wouldn't. You were off doing big-girl things. If you asked Mom …"

"No, please. I don't want to know."

Tony laughed. "It wasn't stealing, I'll give you that much, although beer was involved. Mom was furious, but Dad was pretty cool about it. She grounded me. He directed me to the basketball program with the PAL. But it does make me somewhat sympathetic with Noah's predicament. I'll talk to him. In fact, how about doing it now?"

"I sent him upstairs. He may be asleep."

"Wake him up if he is. I think it would be a good idea if we did this tonight."

Catherine never found out exactly what her brother said to her son; all she knew was when Noah got off the phone, he was considerably less defiant. He even apologized a bit more convincingly about what he'd done. Even if he only did it because his Uncle Tony told him he had to, it made her felt a little better.

Chapter 11

Over the next few days, Catherine and Noah hammered out a working arrangement. He would spend his days until school started in her office with his iPad and a willingness to do errands for anyone in the office who asked. She rescinded the babysitter threat. He agreed that, when school started, he'd come directly home at the end of his day without any detours and call her when he got there. She agreed not to say anything to his friends or tell the school what had happened. But soccer and hanging out with his friends were still off the table, at least for now.

The missing piece was the big one—finding a program to help Noah and give him something positive and productive to do in community service as a penance. Catherine followed up on the suggestions she got from her brother, whose years as a cop in Philly made him a good resource. But every program she contacted had waiting lists for those who had not been sent by the juvenile court. Catherine was almost sorry Noah hadn't been arrested, charged, and processed through the system. At least if he had, she might have an easier time getting him into some kind of program.

She found a counselor to talk to them both, which helped her. Noah wasn't too impressed. Although the counselor said her son was more open when he was there alone, Catherine wasn't sure he was truly cooperating.

She and Dominic went back to their original lobby-and-elevator relationship. He seemed okay with it. She wasn't. She now knew how much she enjoyed his company and his sense of humor. She knew how ready she had been to finally fling herself into his arms and his bedroom.

But Noah was her first priority. If having to put Dominic on hold meant he'd write her off as a missed opportunity, there was nothing she could do about it. She hated seeing him in the building with unfamiliar women. So far when it had happened, he'd always introduced the women, making sure she'd known they were business contacts. It was almost as if he'd known what she'd been thinking.

However, she was sure it couldn't last forever.

• • •

It was like being mired in puberty again with a crush on a girl he couldn't have. Dominic saw Catherine at least once a day, sometimes more. He swore he knew when she'd been in the elevator from the lingering scent of her citrusy-sweet, tangy perfume. They had coffee every now and again, grabbed a quick lunch in the deli once. But she was distracted, not quite there when they talked, not the warm, funny, and sensual woman who'd given him hell on the way to the shore and who'd kissed him in the park like she'd wanted more.

He knew Catherine had planned to bring her son to the office every day until school started, so he wasn't surprised to see Noah around the building, toting coffee and bringing boxes back from the print shop. They didn't speak. Well, Noah didn't. He avoided eye contact and never acknowledged Dominic's greetings.

Catherine told him she hadn't found a place for her son in a program for kids in trouble. Until she did, Dominic was sure his chances of seeing her outside work hours were dim. He knew she was right—sorting things out with Noah had to take priority—but understanding it didn't make it any easier to be patient.

The opera gala was coming up soon. He hadn't said anything to remind her of his invitation for the event, afraid if he brought it up, she'd cancel outright. If she hadn't definitely said "no," he figured he could hold onto the slender hope it might work out. Although he couldn't see how anything was going to change any time soon. The way things were going, he'd be sitting alone in a box at the Academy of Music wondering what it would have been like to have her with him.

He'd put out feelers to everyone he could think of who might know of a program to help Noah, hoping he could find something both Catherine and her son would accept. But in spite of knowing the workings of the city as thoroughly as he understood the mechanics of his car, in spite of having contacts with most of the major players in business, politics, and the non-profit sector, he'd come up dry on a solution to break through this impasse.

Then a board member of a nonprofit, a former client, called. Dominic had already checked out the program for Noah, only to find it had a long waiting list for participants who weren't sent there by the court. But the board had a favor to ask of Dominic, which just might change everything.

There was always one place in the program for a kid recommended by a board or staff member, and the slot had just opened up when a participant had "graduated." Dominic explained the situation with Noah without naming names but with enough detail to persuade the board member that, with a simple swap of favors, everyone might be able to get what they wanted. The board could get what the program needed. Noah would have a place in the best program in Philly. Catherine would lose the stress from her beautiful face, and Dominic might have her back in his life.

For the first time in weeks, things might be falling into place for all of them. There were only a couple items left to do. Getting a sullen teenager to go along with his plan was first.

Two days later, Dominic saw Noah waiting in the coffee shop, apparently for an order to take upstairs to his mother's office, and took the chance to see if he could get that agreement.

"Noah, you're just the person I wanted to see." He put his hand on the boy's shoulder as he came up behind him only to have it shaken off.

Noah didn't turn around; instead he continued to face a stunned-looking barista who'd never seen anyone ignore Dominic that way. "Whaddaya want?"

"First, I'd like to see your face so I know you're really listening to me."

After hesitating for a long moment, Noah complied. "Okay, I'm listening."

"Thank you. I'd like to talk to you for about five minutes."

"I'm picking up coffee for some people in Mom's office. I can't."

"It'll take the barista at least five minutes to make ..." He looked to the man making the drinks who held up eight fingers in response to the unspoken question. "Make eight drinks. We have time."

"They don't want people hanging around here talking."

"I own the building, Noah. It's fine."

"Right. I forgot how important you are."

Nice going, Russo. Exactly the wrong way to approach a sulking teenager. Try again.

"I just need a few minutes, please. How about joining me here?" Dominic indicated the closest table. He sat and invited Noah to do the same. Instead, the boy stood next to the table as if prepared to flee at a moment's notice. "I hear your mom's been looking for a community service program you might like."

Noah shrugged. "I guess."

"There's a program I know about. It might be a good match for you."

There was no response and no glimmer of interest in Noah's eyes.

With nothing to lose at this point, Dominic plowed ahead, undeterred. "It involves working with the adults on staff and a volunteer mentor, an older kid who's also had a scrape or two with authority. The community service part of it's pretty varied—helping coach sports for younger kids, working with environmental groups on river cleanup projects, volunteering in schools. There are lots of different opportunities to—"

"Why do you want to help me?" Noah interrupted. "You don't even know me."

"I know something about you through your mom. And I know she's been stressed out about finding a good program for you."

"Then you're not trying to help me, you're trying to impress Mom." It wasn't a question. It was a statement, a resentful sounding one.

"I want to help both of you."

"Yeah, right." Noah all but snorted his disbelief. "Mom's talked to every program in town and can't find an opening. Why would you be any better at it than she's been?"

"This program has been a client of mine in the past. A couple days ago, a member of the board of directors asked me to help with something. I told him I'd swap favors."

"What'll you have to do for them?"

"I'll help them raise money for the program."

"Like my mom does sometimes? Are you as good as she is?"

"That's not what I want to talk about right now."

Noah persisted with his questions, shifting his weight from foot to foot. "Because you aren't? Or because you think you're better? Which one?"

"We're both good at what we do. Now how about we get back to what I was talking about." He caught Noah's gaze with his, hoping the intensity of what he was about to say was visible. "Look, I know what it's like to get into trouble. How it feels. When I was thirteen, fourteen years old, I messed up and someone helped me. I'm just passing along the help I got."

"How'd you mess up?" For the first time, Noah showed some sign of interest.

"Fighting."

"Like arguing with the teacher?"

"No, like beating up on kids. I almost got thrown out of school because of it. But a school counselor got me interested in graphic art and writing. It became more important to me than fighting. So important, it's how I've made my living all my adult life. I'm not saying the same thing'll happen to you, but isn't it worth a shot to see if something could interest you more than getting in trouble?"

By this time, Noah had slid into the chair across the table from Dominic and was leaning forward, the signs of interest on his face now strong. "You really got in trouble fighting? You don't look like the type. No offense, man, but ..."

"Noah, can we focus on the main question? I'll arm wrestle you some other time if you want me to prove how strong I am."

"You'd help me because someone helped you?"

"Yes."

Noah seemed to be mulling it over in his head, watching Dominic, trying to sort it all out. "Okay, if I decide to let you help, what do I have to do?"

"You don't *have* to do anything. But if you're interested, Google 'Kid-2-Kid' the 'two' is the number and ..."

"My Uncle Tony told me about that program. He said it was the best in Philly but it was really tough to get into unless you'd been sent there by the court."

From the expression on Noah's face, Dominic knew he'd scored by aligning himself with Catherine's brother, who the boy adored. He almost did an entirely out of character fist pump at his luck.

"Your Uncle Tony is correct on both counts. But I think I can make it happen for you. Take a look at the website. Think about it. Talk to your mom or your uncle. Decide what you want to do then give me a call." He pulled a business card from his jacket pocket and handed it to Noah.

"You're not gonna tell my mom what you think I should do?"

"This is not my decision, it's yours. If you or your mom have questions, I can try to answer them, but you have to decide this on your own." He pursed his lips for a moment. "But there's one thing I will do. If you seriously consider this program, seriously enough to convince your mom you mean it, I'll see if I can get her to lift the ban on soccer. You don't have to enter the program if you decide it's not right for you, but you do have to give it a fair chance."

"Can you make her do that?"

"No one can make her do it. All I can do is try to convince her she should think about it." He glanced over at the coffee bar, nodded, and rose from the chair. "Your order's ready. How about I walk with you and call the elevator so you don't have to juggle everything while you push the button."

Chapter 12

Dominic knew intervening in Noah's life was risky. He was not a relative. The boy was a vulnerable teenager. A kid who resented his mother dating. A son who still wanted his parents back together and who was willing to court trouble to get their attention. But as he told Noah, Dominic owed it to the counselor who'd helped him to pass the help along. He'd taken the chance, and now he waited to see what the fallout of his coffee shop intervention would be.

He got a phone call the Monday after his conversation with Noah that relieved him of most of his concerns about what he'd done.

"Hi, Dominic? This is … ah … this is Noah. Noah Bennett."

"Noah. How's it going?"

"Okay, I guess." Long pause. "You said to call when, you know, I'd talked to Mom and everything. I did. Yesterday. We looked at the Kid-2-Kid website. I think I want to try it. We talked to Uncle Tony and he's really in favor of it."

"I'm glad you took it seriously. I'll contact the director today and tell him you're interested. When I talked to him before, I didn't give him details, only said I might have a good candidate for the program. Is it okay if I give him your name and home phone number so he can call and get the ball rolling?"

"Yeah, sure. That's okay." There was silence on the other end of the line for a long moment. "About the other thing …"

"As soon as we're finished here, I'll go down to your mother's office and talk to her about soccer. Like I said before, I can't promise she'll agree, but I'll try my best."

"Thanks."

"You're welcome."

More silence. Noah didn't hang up. He seemed to have something more to say but didn't know how to say it.

"Anything else we need to talk about?" Dominic prodded.

"No. Well, yeah. I guess so." Dominic heard a deep intake of breath on the other end of the line before Noah continued. "I'm sorry I was rude to you. You know, before."

"Apology accepted."

"You haven't been around since then, and I kinda wondered if it was because of me."

"Not in the way you mean, Noah, it isn't. Your mom's been worried about you and needed to make sure things got straightened out before she thought about going out again. I agreed with her."

"Well, if you want to, you know, take her to dinner or something, it would be okay with me. I promised Uncle Tony and her I wouldn't be an asshat again."

Dominic was glad this was a phone call and not a face-to-face conversation. He was having a hard time not smiling at the earnestness in the teen's voice. "Thanks. If she's interested, I'm sure she'll let me know."

"And if you take her out, I could, you know, say thank you in person when you came to pick her up."

"Just stick it out with Kid-2-Kid. That's all the thanks I want."

• • •

"I just talked to Noah—he said he told you he's going to give the program a try." Catherine came from behind her desk with a huge smile on her face. She threw her arms around him. "Thank you so much. You have no idea what this means to me. To Noah and me."

"He got to you faster than I could run the steps." Dominic ducked his head and kissed her. *Lord, this woman tasted good. If he didn't make this kiss short and sweet, he'd forget he was here for Noah, not for himself.* "I think it'll be good for him."

"My brother thinks you walk on water. He says it's exactly where Noah belongs, and he's grateful to you for making it happen." She looked up at him with a curious expression on her face. "Noah said you have to do a favor for the board of directors in exchange for getting him in—what is it?"

"Nothing much. Don't worry about it."

She planted the flat of her hands on his chest and pushed away from him a little. "Dominic, what did you promise? Tell me."

"Some pro bono work." He tried pulling her back into an embrace but she resisted.

"Doing?"

"Raising money."

"You might as well spill the whole thing, Russo. I'll keep asking until you do."

Accompanied with a shoulder shrug he said, "I agreed to raise three quarters of a million in the next month to shore up their sagging capital expansion drive."

She whistled softly. "A lot to raise in a short time. Can I help?"

"You don't have to, but I wouldn't turn help down. However, just so you know ..."

"I understand what pro bono means, Dominic."

"No, I was about to say, just so you know, there's another price for you to pay." Dominic tried to look sinister and mysterious.

"What price? Are you going to auction me off or something to help with the fundraising?"

"Interesting idea. One I hadn't thought of. I'd probably get a damn good price for you, and if some rich foreigner won the bid for you and whisked you to parts unknown, I'd get rid of my competition all in one transaction." He paused as if actually considering it. "No, I'll go with my other idea. It's a little less dramatic and definitely more legal. I want you to reconsider your decision to make Noah give up soccer this fall."

He wasn't sure if she looked confused or angry. "Why would I? It's the only thing I can do to punish him that matters to him."

"I know, but he needs to run off the energy every kid his age has. He'll be happier and so will you if you let him."

"Was this some kind of deal he made with you? He told you if you'd talk me into letting him play, he'd go into the Kid-2-Kid program?"

"No, other way around. I told him I'd make a run at you if he'd consider the program. He didn't have to sign up. He only had to take an honest look at it. He did so I'm here."

"Relying on your legendary charm, were you, to make me buckle?"

"Legendary, huh? I knew I was good, but I had no idea I'd reached legendary status."

"Your attempt at modesty is impressive if not exactly believable."

"So can I get you to lighten up on the soccer ban, or do I have to use more of that charm you mentioned? I can be very persuasive when I put my mind to it, as you might recall."

She blushed, and he realized she might be remembering their first kiss when he had said something similar.

"I only meant I still have the florist's number," he said, enjoying the blush now getting redder by the moment.

"Please, not roses again. And I didn't say I wasn't going to listen to you. I was only trying to appear as though I have some ability to resist you. Which apparently I don't. If you really think it matters so much, I'll let him start practice. But if he gets in trouble one more time, or if his grades drop, or if he screws up working with the program …"

"I understand and so will he, I'm sure."

"Well, shall I tell him or will you?"

"You're the one changing the rules. You tell him." He dropped another kiss on her forehead and was about to leave.

"And, uh, Dominic? Is the invitation still open for the opera next Friday?"

"Absolutely." He hoped the relief he felt didn't show in his voice.

"I have a new dress and a pair of Louboutins I want to wear." She was grinning now.

"So it's about the clothes, not the opera itself?"

"Well, maybe a little to do with the opera."

"Or going out with me?"

"It has a lot to do with that."

"Pick you up at seven."

Chapter 13

Catherine inspected herself in a full-length mirror, turning first one way, then the other. *Oh, yeah. This is the dress for tonight.* The top of her sleeveless, red dress draped in a crisscross over her chest, forming a V emphasizing but not displaying too much of her breasts. The formfitting skirt, which ended in a hem like a mermaid's tail, barely reached her knees. Last but not least expensive, were black-and-white-striped Louboutins, the soles the same color as her dress. She'd bought them as a reward for moving into the new office space with the big guns in her industry, and this was the first chance she'd had to wear them.

Her hair was blown out into waves framing her face and drifting onto her shoulders. Dangly earrings with tiny crystals on fine gold chains brushed her neck.

She'd spent more time than she wanted to admit planning what she would wear, wanting everything about the evening to be perfect. Going to the opera gala was like something from a fairy tale and she was Cinderella. It all had to be just right, which she knew was "Goldilocks," not "Cinderella," but she was in such a good mood, mixing fairy tales didn't bother her.

Even Noah had gotten into the act, surprising her by giving her advice on which earrings he liked best. His opposition to her seeing Dominic seemed to have withered away, probably because Dominic had gone to bat for him over the ban on soccer. In truth, she didn't care why her son was so cooperative. She was just relieved he was.

The doorbell rang as she was about to put on lipstick. Dominic was early, as if he were as eager for the evening to begin as she was. Tucking the tube of lipstick into her evening purse, she hurried down the steps as fast as her shoes would let her.

When she opened the door, she was unprepared for what she saw. Dominic in a business suit was impressive; Dominic in jeans was hot. But Dominic in black tie was magnificent, George Clooney gorgeous. No, better than George. George was off someplace with his wife, and Dominic was standing in front of her.

She gulped, licked her lips, trying to moisten her mouth so she could speak, and made an attempt to get her brain circuits firing enough to find words—any words—someplace in her overheated brain.

"Oh, my God," she said when she could put words together coherently. "Now I know why black tie was invented. The tailors were waiting for you to come along to wear it."

Stunned by how handsome he looked, she'd been blocking his way into the house. But when she stepped back to allow him to enter, he didn't move. Belatedly she realized he had been staring as hard at her as she'd been at him. With his intense dark eyes, he swept down her body, lingering on her neck, then on her breasts, on her legs, then back up to her face. All the while grinning in that sinfully sensuous way he had, melting the core of her into something hot and squishy.

When he finally did move, it was to put one hand on her face and an arm around her waist so he could pull her against him. "I think black tie was invented as a backdrop for a beautiful woman in a red dress who takes my breath away." He ran his thumb over her lower lip. "Mother of God, never in my life have I wanted to kiss anyone so badly."

"Then why don't you?"

He didn't wait to be asked twice.

• • •

It seemed like it had been months since he'd kissed her, really kissed her, not just some sweet peck on the cheek when they parted after having coffee or a reassuring kiss on the forehead to try and smooth away the frown lines. He'd been thinking about this moment ever since she'd said yes to accompanying him tonight. Knew at some point he'd have the chance to cup the back of her neck, run his hand down her spine, hold her tight against his body. He'd thought he'd have to wait until the end of the evening, but here she was demanding he kiss her now. Just as he wanted to do.

Her mouth was soft and sweet, tasting of mint and possibilities. When she sighed against his mouth, he began to slowly stroke her tongue with his, reveling in the feel of her response. He nipped at her lower lip, and she did the same to his. Pulling her closer to him, he hugged her hips against the erection beginning to push against his zipper.

Her dress was cut low in the back; he could touch her soft, warm skin. He wanted to find out if her skin was that smooth, that hot, every place. She had insinuated her arms under his jacket and was holding him tight. If they kissed for a few more moments, maybe she would pop the studs in his shirt so her hands could touch his bare chest. He could press his hands to her breasts, then they could …

The moment of insanity passed. He reluctantly ended the kiss, turned her face away from his, and held her with her head on his chest for a few moments before saying, "We better stop now or we'll never get to the opera."

She giggled. It was a lovely sound, one he didn't think very many people heard. He loved being one of those lucky people.

"You're right. Let me get my wrap and purse, and I'll be ready to go."

They were almost to the sidewalk when he realized kissing her had made him miss something. "You didn't say goodbye to Noah. And I didn't say hi to him."

"He's with his dad until Sunday. Last-minute thing, as usual."

With his dad for the weekend. Dominic's heartbeat ratcheted up at the thought of what it might mean.

When they got to the Escalade, he could see from the look on Jack's face that his driver was gobstruck, too. "Wow, Catherine. You look great."

She smiled, allowed him to help her into the car and said, "Thank you, Jack. It's one of those 'I feel pretty' nights. I'm flattered you noticed."

"I'd have to be blind not to notice."

Dominic slid onto the seat beside her. "Enough. I don't employ you to flirt with my date."

"Not flirting, Dominic. Only telling it like it is. Don't you agree she's a knockout?"

"I already told her how beautiful she is. How beautiful she always is." Dominic took her hand and squeezed it.

"There's hope for you yet. Keep it up so I get to see her again," Jack said as he started the engine.

"And once again, you two, I'm here, I'm not asleep, and I'm embarrassed. Can we get to the Academy?" Catherine asked.

In unison, the two men said, "Yes, ma'am," and Jack headed out.

•••

The line of cabs, limos, and luxury cars trying to reach the Grand Old Lady of Locust Street was long. Creeping along for ten minutes got them less than a block closer to the entrance, so Dominic and Catherine got out and walked.

It was a crisp fall night. The sidewalk was crowded with men and women in formal dress, all headed in the same direction, an air of celebration about them. Dominic offered Catherine his arm. She thanked him for helping her navigate the sidewalk in stilettos. In truth, he hadn't been thinking of her. He'd been thinking of himself. With her arm tucked through his, she was so close he could feel the warmth of her body, smell her perfume, touch her hand, her arm, her shoulder. Her breast was pressed against his arm.

And without trying, there he was, back in her entry hall when he'd felt those breasts against his chest. It wouldn't do to have the same reaction he'd had then. Not here, in front of her and this crowd of politically connected, culturally interested, and socially prominent Philadelphians. He had to clear his mind. Think of the music they'd be hearing inside, not the music he'd heard when she'd moaned in his arms and molded her body to his as they'd kissed. The sound of what he could only hope he'd hear when he had her in his bed. The sound … oh, hell, he needed something to distract him or this would be more embarrassing than anything since high school.

He landed on, "I was thinking. Since you don't have to be home early, maybe we could do something later, after the reception to honor our guest from Italy."

"Did you have something in mind?"

"A drink? Dancing? What would you like to do?"

"Dessert, maybe."

Apparently he hadn't told her about the desserts waiting for them at the reception. Either that or she was seriously addicted to sweets. But he wasn't going to argue about it. If she wanted more dessert, he'd get it for her. "Great. Anything specific?"

"Well, I was thinking … maybe … maybe tiramisu would be nice."

He wasn't sure if he would first choke on his tongue or trip on a crack in the pavement. He stopped in the middle of the sidewalk to avoid one and swallowed hard to avert the other. The crowd of opera patrons surging around them disappeared into some other dimension, and he could see only her big, dark eyes full of amusement. "Tiramisu? Do you mean …?"

She lowered her thick eyelashes as if abashed, although her wicked smile said something else. "Have you forgotten already? The code?"

"Hell, no, I haven't forgotten. But I wasn't expecting … I mean, are you sure?" He frowned as an unwanted thought crossed his mind. "You don't think you owe me something, do you? For the evening? For getting Noah in the program?"

"Don't insult us both, Dominic. Of course I don't." He opened his mouth to respond, but she went on. "I was this close," she held up one hand with her thumb and forefinger a half-inch apart, "this close to saying it when we were in Fairmount Park before all hell broke loose. I've been waiting since then for another chance. Tonight's the first time it's been possible. Are you turning me down?"

"Do you think I've lost my mind? Of course I'm not turning you down. But, Jesus, Catherine, your timing leaves something to be desired. Couldn't you have waited until after the performance? Between the kiss in your entryway and this, you have now presented me with the one thing that would deter me from hearing this performance. I want to grab you, call Jack, and get to my apartment in the next ten minutes."

She laughed as she looked over his shoulder. "We can't. There are at least three people coming toward us who look like they want to talk to you."

As if to prove her point, the mayor approached. "Dominic, good to see you. I hoped you'd be here. I wanted to thank you for the work you did for the Police Athletic League."

"Nice to see you, too, Mister Mayor. And thank you. We enjoyed doing the campaign." He put his hand at the small of Catherine's back. "Do you know Catherine Bennett? Catherine, Mayor Thompson."

The mayor took her hand and smiled. "Of course I know the beautiful Ms. Bennett. She did the rollout for the Green Tech incubator space. Nice to see you again, Catherine."

"Lovely evening, isn't it, Mayor?" Catherine asked as she shook his hand.

"It is, indeed." The mayor's eyebrows went a good distance toward his hairline as he smirked. "So, which one of you is scoping out the competition by spending the evening with the other? It strikes me as something you'd be more likely to do, Dominic."

"Sorry to disappoint you, Mister Mayor, but this is purely personal."

"Don't blame you. I'd ask her out, too, if I had an understanding wife." The mayor's attention was distracted by something he was looking at beyond the couple. "You'll have to forgive me. I see my most obstreperous council member haranguing a perfectly innocent supporter of mine. I need to ride to the rescue. Enjoy the evening."

"Purely personal, is it?" Catherine said when the mayor was out of earshot. "And here I thought I was such a threat to your business you had to keep me close—you know, the keep-your-friends-close-and-your-enemies-closer thing?"

He kissed her temple. "Never your enemy, Catherine. And more than your friend, I hope."

She looked up with such desire in her eyes, his knees almost buckled. "I hope so too, Dominic."

They made their way into the Academy and up to a box that seated a half dozen people. When she asked who else would be joining them, he said no one would. He liked to be alone when he came to the opera, not distracted by other people who wanted to talk during the performance, which too many people did. And his financial support of the opera gave him the luxury of getting first crack at the good seats.

He let her choose her seat, then moved another of the gilt chairs close to hers. The buzz of the crowd grew louder as people began to fill up the main floor below and the boxes around them. Dominic used the cover of the noise to kiss Catherine's shoulder and whisper, "However, I don't object to being distracted with conversation before the opera begins. In fact, I have a question I'd like to ask you."

"Sure. What do you want to know?"

"How do you like to be seduced?"

Her startled reaction was rewarding. "What?"

"I think I was clear about my request. How do you like to be …?"

"Why are you asking?"

"Because I want to get it right. There are a lot of ways to seduce a woman and …"

"And you know them all?" The tone of her voice was amused even though he'd been going for excited.

"No, but it's much more enjoyable when both parties agree on what they like." He traced a line over her collarbone with his forefinger. "For example, I like the feel of your skin. Do you like to be seduced with touch?" His finger moved from her collarbone down to the top of her breast. "Like this?"

Her sharp intake of breath was all he needed to continue his explorations. With the softest of touches, he moved from her chest, up her neck to her chin then to the curve of her ear and the soft lobe. He could see her nipples peaking through the drape of her dress.

"Or shall I *tell* you how soft your skin is? Seduce you with words. By saying how much I want to touch your breasts the way I'm touching your ear. How much I want to see if your thighs are as soft and smooth as …"

"Dominic, please."

"Please, what, *cara*?"

"Please … I don't … I don't know." She moved restlessly in her seat, tried to put space between them, but he wouldn't let her. "Don't tease me like this."

"I'm not teasing. I'm doing research for later." He kissed her temple. "How about seduction by kissing?" He began to give her light, butterfly kisses from her temple to her cheek, to her ear and her neck. His hand moved across the span of her waist, and he pulled her against him, her back to his chest. With the other hand he moved her hair to one side so he could nibble at her neck and shoulder. He knew from the way she was breathing, from the way her head was thrown back, he'd achieved his goal. She was excited.

Then the lights went down and the orchestra began to play the overture.

• • •

Jesus, what the hell was she supposed to do now? It was her turn to want to call Jack and get to Dominic's apartment as quickly as they could. Never had she been so completely and thoroughly aroused with the brush of a mouth on her skin, a soft touch or the whisper of words. The man was living up to Melody's nickname, and they were still fully dressed and in a box at the opera. Maybe she was taking on more than she could handle with him. Maybe Melody was right about that.

Focus. She had to focus on what was happening on stage. Dominic didn't make it easy. Although he had released her and settled back into his seat, he still had his arm around the back of her chair and was moving his thumb up and down on the back of her neck. Little sparks were constantly igniting on her skin. Her breasts ached, and a curl of desire wound its way through her body.

If she was going to survive the evening, she had to do something. She moved forward slightly, took his arm from around her, and placed his hand on her knee, where she held it in as safe a place as she could find. Not that there was much safe on a body tingling from his touch.

The expression on his face was both smug and sensual. "Is something wrong, Catherine?"

"If I'm going to enjoy this performance, it would be better to have your hand where I can see it. Maybe even control it so it doesn't … can't … do what it's been doing to me."

He leaned over and whispered, "Touching you does the same thing to me. And I like it."

"Shouldn't we respect the performers enough to pay attention? After all, you paid a fortune for this box."

He smiled. "Ah, yes. Respect for the performers. You're right." He raised her hand to his mouth and kissed it. "I'll behave."

"Thank you." She knew she sounded schoolmarmish, but it worked. Now she might get through the opera without melting into a puddle of lust at his feet.

The man was sex on legs, sex on a chair, sex in an SUV, sex wherever he was.

Chapter 14

During the first intermission, Dominic and Catherine had left their box for a glass of wine, but the constant interruption of people who wanted to talk to her date convinced Catherine to stay in her seat during the last break between acts. And maybe, while he was gone, think of something other than how damned hot the man was.

But she didn't have a chance to catch her breath. A steady stream of people "dropped by" the box, apparently to see who Dominic was with. At least, that's what it seemed like. One client of hers who came by did everything but ask outright why Catherine was with her competitor. Several acquaintances subtly made sure Catherine knew they were surprised to see whom she was with. Others said they were only there to "say hi" to Dominic, though they could have seen from anyplace in the Academy that he wasn't in the box. She felt like she was being inspected by half the audience, whether to see if she was worthy of Dominic or crazy for being with him, she didn't know.

After the tenth, fifteenth, twentieth—she lost count—person "just came by to give my regards to Dominic," she'd had it. Since she didn't have the materials in her purse for a sign saying, "He's in the lobby," she decided escape was the next best option. She went to the ladies room. Surely no one would bother her there.

Locked inside a stall where she vowed to remain until she heard the signal to end the intermission, she thought she was safe. Then a conversation between two women waiting in line whose voices she didn't recognize floated over the top of the door.

"Did you see Dominic Russo up there in his box? Showing off with yet another woman. He didn't even wait until the lights went out to kiss her."

"Of course I saw him. He makes sure we all see him, doesn't he? I mean, buying a whole box for himself and his bimbo. Really?"

"He's always up there by himself, showing off his money or his women. I don't recognize this one. But then, I don't recognize most of them. For a man who knows all the right people, he doesn't seem to care about the woman he's with. All he cares about, I swear, is whether she looks good on his arm for the event and in his bed afterward."

"This one won't last any longer than the others, I guarantee. He goes through women faster than I go through tissues in ragweed season."

There was a round of nasty laughs, which abruptly ceased when Catherine opened the stall door and, head high, walked to the washbasin. She was gratified to see the embarrassed expressions on the faces of the two women. Even more gratified to see the looks of horror when she ripped tissues from the box on the sink and dropped them into their hands saying, "Here, in case you ran out what with all the ragweed around. The last act's a tearjerker."

She strode out of the ladies room without looking back, but once she was out of sight of the door she slowed, then stopped and slumped against the wall. This was not the fairy tale evening she'd hoped for. She had to face facts—she wasn't a princess, and Dominic Russo sure as hell wasn't a knight on a white horse. He was a man who dated women who were useful to him. He'd even told her that on the way back from their lunch at the shore. Although the ugly stepsisters in the ladies room certainly thought he used women for something other than business.

Did she really think putting herself in danger of having her ego trashed and her heart broken by a man who people talked about like those women had was a good idea?

•••

Something had happened. Dominic could tell by the look on Catherine's face, the tension in her shoulders, the way she flinched when he touched her. When she moved her chair away from his, he asked, "Is something wrong? Are you okay?"

"I'm fine." She sat facing forward, not looking at him when she answered.

"No, you're not. No woman I've ever known has said 'I'm fine' that way and meant anything other than she wasn't fine at all."

"And, of course, you've known enough women to have a statistically accurate basis for your observation."

"Where the hell did that comment come from?" He grasped her shoulders and turned her toward him. "What's going on, Catherine? Talk to me, before the act starts."

"It doesn't matter. Enjoy the opera." She shook off his hands and moved her chair even farther away from his. He thought he could see tears beginning in her eyes, eyes with a frightened look in them.

The lights dimmed; the crowd hushed; the act was about to begin.

He could see the muscle in her jaw clenching and unclenching, as if she were angry. But the fear in her eyes and the tears he was sure were starting there said something else.

He scooted his chair close to her and whispered, "Catherine, what's upset you?"

She whispered back, "Hush. The curtain's going up."

"The hell with the curtain. If you don't tell me what's going on, I swear to God I'll hoist you over my shoulder and take you to the lobby. Maybe then you'll tell me."

"Is that how you treat all your bimbos? You caveman them until they do what you want?"

"My bimbos? What the hell …?"

A chorus of "shushes" came from the adjoining boxes.

He stood and yanked at her arm, whispering, "We're going out to the hall, and I'm getting to the bottom of this." He could tell she was not happy about his demand, but she was apparently even less happy about making a scene, because she followed him.

Once they were outside the box, he asked again, "What happened while I was gone to piss you off so badly?"

She leaned against the wall and stared at the ceiling for an agonizingly long time before asking, "Do you ever bring the same woman to two events like this?"

"I have no idea. I've never thought about it. Why?"

"Do you pick your dates based on how good they'll look on your arm or in your bed?"

"Enough stupid questions. Get to what happened."

There was another lapse of time followed by a deep breath and then one long, emotional sentence. "I left the box because everyone kept 'accidently' dropping by to make sure I knew how many people had seen us together or maybe to see who the latest Dominic Russo conquest was or maybe figure out why it was me here and not someone else—someone better—I don't really know why they were all there, but they were. People I haven't seen in years. A client or two. People I've never met in my life."

She paused to take a breath. "Anyway, when I couldn't take the attention anymore, I went to the ladies room hoping to escape, but while I was in the stall, two women were talking about how you never date the same woman twice, how all the women you date are bimbos, what a shame it is you have such bad taste in women ..."

"*That's* what this is about? That kind of crap?" He ran his fingers through his hair as he paced in front of her. "Jesus, Catherine, I told you before. Most of the women I've gone out with have been business acquaintances, hardly bimbos. And how could you even think I consider you a bimbo? Or that I'm interested in you for only one date? I've been trying to get you to go out with me for months. Does it sound like I've got some hidden plan to get rid of you after tonight?"

She was twisting her fingers in front of her, looking now at the floor, the walls, anyplace but at him.

"I can't believe you'd listen to bullshit gossip," he continued. "And I'm pissed you still think me capable of something like that. So pissed I feel like dragging you off to some dark corner and kissing you silly to show you exactly how I feel about you."

Now she looked at him, seeming to fight a small smile. "I thought you said you didn't drag women off to janitors' closets anymore."

"I said I feel like it. I didn't say I would do it." He stopped pacing in front of her. "Why in the world would you let a bunch of catty bitches spoil the evening?"

"I was spooked. I wasn't prepared to be the object of such overwhelming interest because I appeared in public with you. I felt hunted, like Kate Middleton was when she first started dating William." She reached for him and he met her halfway, grasping her hands with both of his. "I have no problem with people paying attention to me professionally. But this, this is different. It's uncomfortable. It made me wonder …" She looked down at the floor again. "I was worried I'd read the whole thing wrong about your interest."

"You didn't read anything wrong. Except about comparing yourself to Kate Middleton. You're more beautiful than she is." With a forefinger, he lifted her face and kissed her gently. "I'm sorry you got run over by my reputation. I should have warned you. I manage to ignore it because at least it means people know who I am, which probably helps my business. It doesn't mean anything otherwise."

"I guess … maybe I overreacted. I did try to warn you how out of practice I am for social events."

Dominic recognized the music coming from inside the Academy announcing one of his favorite parts of the last act. "If we can finish this later, I'd like to hear the end of the opera." He kissed her as he opened the door to the box. "We both might find the lives of fictional characters easier to deal with for a while."

Chapter 15

The only way Catherine had expected to go from the top of the mountain to the bottom of the canyon in the course of the evening was through the music. She knew she'd follow the characters on stage on such a journey; she had no idea she'd go there in real life.

Was she so accustomed to the well-worn ruts of her normal routine that she'd forgotten how to cope with the unexpected? Was it because she'd never been associated with someone who everyone either knew or wanted to know?

Or did it run deeper? Was she still afraid of his motives? Wondering if he had some reason for pursuing her other than wanting to enjoy her company? Even more worrisome, was she still so afraid of being hurt that she'd push away the most attractive man who'd ever paid attention to her?

She almost wished he'd made good on his threat to take her off into a dark corner and kiss her silly. When he kissed her, she knew exactly what she wanted—him. Any way she could have him. Every way she could have him. When they were alone together—or even in the SUV with Jack driving—it was easy to be in the moment, not worried about anything. But when they were out in public, as they were tonight, it was obvious she was working without a net.

•••

The opera ended with a standing ovation for the cast. Dominic put his arm around Catherine and whispered, "Do you want to leave now and avoid the reception?"

She shook her head, still clapping. "And give up the chance to meet the star? Of course not."

They walked next door to the lobby of the Kimmel Center where the reception was already underway. Half a dozen people greeted Dominic as soon as he was in the door. He hesitated before letting one of his clients drag him off, but Catherine, too, had been immediately commandeered by someone she'd greeted with a big smile. He tried to follow both the conversation he was in and her progress across the room, but a heated discussion of the election the following year diverted his attention, and he lost track of her. Unable to see her in the crowd, he excused himself and went looking for her. A repeat of the conversation she'd overheard in the ladies room was the last thing he wanted for her.

He shouldn't have been concerned. She was obviously enjoying herself—with the guest of honor. The tenor was laughing at something she said, touching her arm, standing a damn sight too close to her for Dominic's comfort.

After making his way to her side, he wrapped his arm around her waist and kissed her on the cheek. "Here you are, *cara*. I thought I'd lost you." He turned to the singer who'd just wowed the audience and put out his hand to introduce himself and compliment the performance. "*Sono Domenico Russo. Eri magnifico stasera. Grazie per la splendida performance.*"

The other man switched to Italian and thanked him for the compliment. "*Grazie, è stato un piacere.*"

"*Vedo che hai conosciuto la mia ragazza.*" Dominic made sure the singer knew the woman he'd been flirting with was taken. By him.

But the tenor wasn't to be put off. He laughed and suggested if she got tired of American men, he'd be interested. "*Se lei stanca di uomini Americani …*"

Catherine interrupted. "English, please."

"I'm sorry, Catherine. I forgot you don't speak Italian. We were saying what an amazing night this has been." He could tell from her face she knew he wasn't telling the whole truth.

"We were also saying how beautiful you are, Catherine. Truly a *bella donna*."

Before Catherine could respond, the chairman of the symphony board approached with several major donors who wanted to meet the star, and Dominic took the opportunity to say *"addio"* to their Italian friend and lead her away. He didn't get far before another of his clients claimed his attention and Catherine went off on her own again.

• • •

It wasn't as bad as she thought it would be. The reception that is. The champagne was excellent, the spread of desserts tempting, and the background music—the tenor's newest CD, she was sure—perfect. As she watched Dominic work the room, Catherine admired how easy and comfortable he was, able to talk to anyone it seemed. Never once looking bored, impatient, or anything but eager to chat with whoever waylaid him in his progression through the crowd. He was the master of schmoozing.

Actually, she did all right herself. There were a number of people there she knew, including a handful of clients who introduced her to their colleagues and friends. She was back at the top of her game, at ease being the president of Bennett and Associates instead of Dominic Russo's latest conquest. She was glad she'd remembered to stick business cards in her purse, and ended up with a few leads on potential clients. Maybe Dominic's approach to marketing wasn't such a bad idea.

To make it perfect, she didn't see either of the two women from the ladies room. She had a nasty attack of smugness, assuming they hadn't donated enough money to get invited to the reception. It felt good. Even though she knew she hadn't either and was only there because Dominic had.

The evening began to wind down after a few remarks from the symphony president and a last round of applause for the guest of honor before he left. Dominic called Jack and asked him to pick them up out front.

As they waited on the sidewalk, Dominic put his arm around her shoulders and hugged her. "I'm glad you were with me this evening. Even our guest agreed that you were the most beautiful woman here. He said if you got tired of American men pretending to be Italian, he'd be happy to show you what a real Italian man was like."

She was sure her nervous laugh told him exactly how surprised she was. "He probably said the same thing about every woman there." She avoided his eyes and moved a few inches out of his embrace.

"I doubt it. He said it in his language, so I understood clearly he was making a play for you."

"Well, whatever he thought, you know the truth—I wasn't the world's best date tonight. I was more like a teenager. Maybe Noah and I have more in common than I thought."

His gaze traveled up and down her body. "Are you telling me you're smuggling out a bottle of champagne under your dress? I don't know where you'd put it."

A sigh this time, rather than a laugh. "No, I meant I acted badly when things didn't go the way I'd expected them to." She looked up at him. "I think I expected too much from the evening." She saw his expression change to concern and hurried to explain. "Oh, not that the opera and the reception weren't wonderful. They were. And you've been patient, more patient than I should expect. It's just that …"

"Just that you've changed your mind about how the evening ends?"

In a wavering voice, she added, "Maybe. I'm not sure. I mean, I still want … it still might be …"

His brown eyes looked intense. "There's no expectation on my part that we end up back at my place, you know."

"Don't you want us to …?" For the first time in her life, her heart, just like the cliché, was in her throat where she could feel it beating so hard she was sure Dominic could hear it.

"That's not what I said—or meant. You know what I want. What I've wanted all along. What do you want? Tonight, I mean," he asked.

"I know what I wanted when the evening started out. But now …"

"Now you're not sure." It wasn't a question. It was a statement.

"I think I am. Maybe. I know what I want when you kiss me. Does that help?"

He smiled. "It soothes my ego quite a bit, yes. But if you're not so certain the rest of the time, then I'll be certain for both of us."

The Escalade pulled up at the curb, and Dominic opened the door and helped Catherine in. When he was settled in the back he said, "We're going to Catherine's house, Jack."

"Whatever you say, boss." And they were off.

The traffic was light and they got to her townhouse quickly. Which was good because they said little, although Dominic kept his arm around her and had urged her to nestle her head into his shoulder, where it was so comfortable she wondered if she—if he—had made the right choice.

When Jack stopped in front of her home, Dominic told him to wait and walked Catherine to the door. He kissed her lightly then asked, "Are you going to work in the morning?"

"Probably. You?"

"Of course. How about lunch? Maybe we should regroup in broad daylight rather than—" he looked at his watch "—at almost one in the morning."

"Lunch works, if you're sure you want to make any more plans with me."

Although he avoided responding to her comment, he said, "Twelve thirty. My office." He kissed her again. "See you then."

"Your office? Not the deli?"

"I promise you a more interesting place to have lunch than the deli." He walked down the steps to the Escalade, leaving her curious, frustrated, and completely unsure what to expect at lunch.

Chapter 16

Catherine didn't sleep well. Her doubts and demons made sure she spent most of the night questioning herself about how she'd handled the evening at the Academy. And the questions were endless. Why had she reacted the way she had when she'd heard those two women gossiping? Was she afraid to put herself out there because she might be hurt? Had the old fear that Dominic wanted to get to know her for some nefarious business reason resurfaced? Or had she been, as Dominic suggested, merely surprised by the gossip about his reputation?

If the questions about herself were difficult to answer, the ones she came up with about Dominic were impossible to figure out. Would what happened at the Academy make him decide she couldn't handle being with him and it was simply not going to work between them? Why hadn't he kissed her good night the way he had kissed her at the beginning of their evening? Was it because he hadn't wanted to start something he wasn't going to be able to finish? Or was it because he wanted to back away from getting any closer to her?

Then there were the big ones: Should she have insisted on going to his place? And how many chances would she have with the first man she'd been interested in since … well, since forever?

No matter how she posed the questions, she couldn't begin to figure out what the right answers were. After all, he was Mister Sex on Legs, and she was "St. Catherine," the woman who'd earned her reputation in high school and college by concentrating on classes, not guys. The few semi-serious relationships she'd had before she'd fallen for Andy Bennett hardly equipped her to deal with someone like Dominic. And since the divorce? *Niente.*

She almost called Tony, knowing with the time difference he might still be awake. But she decided it was too embarrassing to consult her little brother about her sex life. Not that she wouldn't have made his week complete with the phone call. After he stopped laughing at her, he'd make her apologize for years of lecturing him about his adventures with women when she was now asking his advice because of that experience.

She wore herself out in frustrating conversations with the little imps who inhabited her mind until she fell asleep about four a.m.

A long shower in the morning helped revive her. So did coffee and knowing she looked good, once she dressed in her favorite clothes. In fact, she took almost as much time getting ready to go to her office as she had getting ready for the opera the night before. No usual Saturday outfit of jeans and T-shirt today. She selected a pair of chocolate brown pants she knew fit her well, a tan, scoop neck crop top that hugged her body in an almost ladylike manner. She even wore her favorite spike heels, which meant she had to drive to work instead of getting her one shot of exercise for the week.

But she wanted to look good. If she couldn't remind Dominic he thought she was worth waiting for, at least she'd walk away with style when he let her go.

Maybe it was self-defense, maybe it was avoidance, but she was able to divert herself all morning with work. In fact, she was so involved with what she was doing, she was almost late for their twelve-thirty date. When she arrived at the fifteenth floor, she discovered an apparently deserted set of offices. Only Dominic was there, working on a laptop, glancing occasionally at a desktop computer or a thick memo. Focused on what he was doing, he didn't seem to realize she was standing in the door to his office, which gave her a chance to admire the scenery, as Melody had so aptly put it. He was in his usual Saturday jeans and Polo shirt. And he must have slept well, because he looked rested. And sexy. Damn. Why did he have to be so attractive?

"Knock, knock" she said. "It's twelve thirty."

He looked up and smiled when he saw her. "Come in. I'm almost finished."

"If you're not ready, I can come back." She motioned toward the hall. "I can even, you know, postpone if you need to."

In a few long strides, he was across the room and had his arms around her as if to make sure she didn't leave. "No, *cara*, don't go. Give me two minutes to get the computers shut down, and we'll have lunch." He returned to his desk after a quick kiss on the top of her head.

She looked around for signs of food. "Do you want me to get something from the deli? Oh, maybe you had something delivered to one of your conference rooms. Or …"

"Patience, Catherine. Two minutes." As he spoke, he clicked on the keyboard of the desktop computer then closed up the laptop. Finished with his work, he led her to the elevators and pulled out a key card.

"You have one more elevator door than we do on our floor," Catherine said. "How come I never noticed it before?"

"Can't answer that. But I can tell you why. The original plan was for a white tablecloth restaurant on this floor with an outdoor space on the roof for eating in nice weather. This elevator was for food deliveries and access. It only opens on the first floor, here, and the roof." He swiped the card and the door opened.

"I wanted this floor for our offices, not a restaurant," he continued. "But the shaft for the elevator was already in. So I took advantage of it and had something added I've always wanted."

As if obeying the wishes of the building owner, the door opened and revealed an urban garden like none Catherine had ever seen. It was more than grass and a few trees to look environmentally correct; it was a little bit of paradise in the middle of the city.

A large, triangular shelter composed of wisteria-covered lattice jutted out from the glass entry to the elevator hall. Flanking a slate floor were huge terra cotta pots with well-established shrubs and annual flowers in them. Two chairs and a table were arranged in the center to take in the view of the urban landscape. On the table was a tray covered with cloth towels. Lunch, she assumed.

A slate path, the pieces interspersed with mossy plants, led to the other side of the roof where the HVAC systems were discretely camouflaged by modestly sized trees now beginning to shed their leaves. On either side of the path were sections of grass bisected by large wooden raised planter boxes with what appeared to be tomatoes, lettuces, and herbs growing in them. She could hear the sounds of a water feature someplace nearby.

"This is amazing. How come I didn't see this when I got the tour of the building from the real estate agent?" Catherine asked.

"Because no one gets to come up here except me and whomever I bring with me. It's my private refuge," Dominic explained.

"And it's perfectly beautiful."

He gestured to the table. "Dave from the deli sent our lunch up. He said he wanted to surprise us, so I'm not sure what it is. But whatever it is, I imagine it'll include the tomatoes and lettuce he grows in those raised beds."

What the deli manager had sent was a Cobb salad with, as predicted, tomatoes and lettuce from the garden in front of them, hard-cooked eggs, avocados, bacon, and blue cheese dressing accompanied by iced tea and fresh-baked rolls. The conversation during lunch was casual and light. Considering the evening before, which her night of sleeplessness had convinced her was a complete disaster, and considering she was unsure what to expect from Dominic, Catherine was surprised it was so easy to keep it going.

But finally, lunch was finished and she needed to broach the embarrassing subject. "About last night—"

He didn't let her finish. "I've thought about it and I think it would be better not to—"

Now it was her turn to interrupt. "What? You think it would be better not to ... what?"

"You're awfully impatient today, Catherine. First, about lunch. Now this."

"*Dannazione*, Russo. Spit it out. If you think we're doomed to have this, whatever it is between us, not work out, I understand. Two dates. Two disasters. If you want go back to coffee and an occasional elevator ride, please, tell me and get it over with."

She hated the smirk on his face. Hated it. Wanted to wipe it off. Kiss it off. Something.

"You do swear in Italian, don't you?" he said. "And you're cranky today. You must not have slept well last night."

"Dominic, so help me ..."

He held up his hands as if to ward off any further words. "I was only going to say I think it would be better not to read too much into what happened. The gossip about my personal life is only slightly annoying to me because I'm used to it. You're not, so it's understandable it might upset you. I should have given you a heads up. I thought what Melody told you about my reputation would have prepared you, but I was wrong."

Stunned into silence, Catherine struggled to find the right words.

"Have I said something you don't agree with?" Dominic asked, his smirk replaced with a slightly worried frown.

She took a deep breath. "Are you saying you still want to hang out with me?"

"I have a bit more than hanging out in mind, but, yes, that's the general idea." He furrowed his brow. "Just one thing. Last night did arouse my curiosity about something. You don't have to if you don't want to, but would you tell me about Noah's father?"

Again, the conversation wasn't going in the direction she'd expected. "I don't mind, although I don't see what Andy has to do with anything." She shrugged. "There's really not much to tell, anyway. We met in college his freshman year. I was two years ahead of him. We dated until I graduated, then reconnected when he was looking for a job. I persuaded my boss to hire him at the PR firm where I was working. We got married, had a baby, got divorced when Noah was almost ten."

"So, you … what … grew apart? Was that the reason for the divorce?"

"Not exactly." She didn't meet his stare, which seemed to be seeing straight into her soul.

"What exactly, if you don't mind telling me."

She did mind. But she had the feeling this was important, maybe in figuring out her reaction at the Academy. "He fell in love with someone else. Someone he'd met in college after I graduated. She reappeared in his life and …" She stopped, reluctant still to admit her husband hadn't been faithful to her.

"And he had an affair?" Dominic prompted.

"Yes, and now he's married to her."

"Did it make you doubt you could trust another man?"

"Maybe. I felt used by Andy, that's for sure. I got him the job he wanted and the son he wanted, but he made me feel that wasn't enough. I wasn't enough." She felt self-conscious talking about herself this way but continued anyway. "It was hard to swallow. I'd been the oldest, most responsible, smartest kid in my family. But somehow he almost convinced me I was a failure, not interesting enough to keep his attention."

"*Almost* convinced you?" He didn't say any more.

"Maybe, when everyone seemed so eager to see who you had brought to the event and those two nasty women talked about all the other women you'd been seen with and I remembered what Melody had said, maybe I thought I wasn't the kind of woman who'd interest you for very long." She stopped to take a breath. "Maybe I didn't want to set myself up for the same thing happening again." She couldn't look at him, afraid of what she might see.

"Don't you think I should have a say in what kind of woman interests me?" His voice was soft, sweet, warm.

"I guess so."

"I know so. And here's what else I know—you're the most interesting woman—most interesting person—I've met in years."

They were both silent for a long moment, neither one looking at the other. Suddenly they each turned to the other and said, almost simultaneously, "Dominic, I—" and "Catherine, I—"

There was laughter from them both, his amused, hers nervous.

"Ladies first," he said.

"Can we do something together tonight, only the two of us? Without the rest of the city of Philadelphia?"

"I was about to ask you if I could make dinner for you tonight at my place. In fact, if you'd like ..." He paused for a moment before adding, "I'd like to cook dinner for you tonight and breakfast for us tomorrow morning."

Chapter 17

Dominic didn't usually invite a woman to his place. His home was like his roof garden—a refuge. But Catherine was different. He'd wanted her there since the first time he'd had lunch with her, and he intended to make tonight as perfect as he could for them.

He knew exactly what to make: his mother's Bolognese sauce. It would take a few hours to simmer while they drank wine and talked. Once the sauce was finished, the pasta would be quick to cook and a salad easy to put together. A bit of wine, an antipasto plate, and the menu was complete. Dessert? He had something in mind for dessert that didn't come from the grocery—or any other—store.

Fortunately, his house cleaning service had been there on Friday so the place was neat, the sheets and towels fresh, and even the windows clean. All he had to do was get the sauce started, arrange a few candles, and cue up Andrea Bocelli on his music system, and his home was ready. He shaved again and changed from jeans to black pants with a white dress shirt. Now all he needed was the woman.

...

Catherine hadn't been this anxious about a date since high school. She was so nervous that she changed her top twice before the time Jack was to pick her up, because she was sure she'd pitted out the two rejects sweating. She tried to blame it on the summer heat, although in her heart she knew it wasn't anything a change in the weather could fix. Twice she'd broken out in a cold sweat thinking about what she'd set herself up for. She'd been so sure she was ready to do this, have her fling. And not with just any man. The king of the deep end of the dating pool she'd told Melody she didn't want to be in. But here she was about to go off the high dive right into it.

It was enough to make anyone sweat.

The cream-colored silk shirt she had on now would probably not make it through the evening either. She was about to change for the third time when she saw looked at the clock. Her ride would be there any minute. She'd have to take a chance with the silk.

Grabbing the messenger bag she decided would be a more subtle way to carry a few toiletries and clean underwear than some sort of overnight bag, she went downstairs where she added the bottle of wine she was taking as a host present and waited for Jack to arrive. She'd resisted the chauffeur service when Dominic suggested he send his car to pick her up. She preferred the freedom to leave whenever she wanted. But Dominic had convinced her to let Jack drive her so she wouldn't have to search for a safe place to leave her car in a neighborhood where parking was tight and car vandalism not unusual.

Sitting in her living room, she wondered if delivering a woman to Dominic was part of Jack's job description and no big thing. *Maybe he's done this before. Maybe when he said Dominic didn't go out much he meant he entertained at home a lot. If she asked, would Jack tell her about them?*

Stop. She was not going to go *there*, to the stupid place where she'd been last night. She was an accomplished professional, not some teenage virgin. She was going to Dominic's for what *she* wanted.

• • •

Jack pulled up in front of another new-looking building, similar enough in design to Dominic's office building for her to wonder if the same architect had designed it. The street-level floor was all glass, with panels of etched abstract designs every yard or so providing light from the outside as well as a degree of privacy for the residents as they walked through the lobby. There were large, green plants placed between the etched-glass panels. The prominent security desk in the center of the white marble lobby staffed by a stern-looking guard was softened somewhat by the oversized color photographs of the city on the wall behind it.

Before she could ask Jack where she was to go he said, "Penthouse, Catherine. The security guard will get the elevator for you."

The penthouse. Naturally. Where else would Dominic Russo live?

In minutes, she was whisked up to another marble lobby. Dominic was waiting, a welcoming smile on his face. Obviously the security guy had called and let him know she was on her way up.

He took her hand and drew her close for a lingering kiss, then took the bottle of wine she offered, thanked her, and led her into his apartment. The room she entered managed to be both visually stunning and comfortable—cozy, even. Floor-to-ceiling glass walls, as in his office, brought light into an open-plan living room and dining room. The interior walls were painted a toasty warm tan. In strategic places on the hardwood floors were large Persian carpets in browns, deep reds, and blues. Two armchairs upholstered in a nubby-looking, dark blue fabric and a brown leather couch were grouped close to a small fireplace set into the corner between the living room and dining room so it was visible from both. Pillows were thrown casually on the couch and the chairs. One wall was hung with art. Another was covered in bookshelves with chairs grouped in front.

The dining room was small, furnished with only a sideboard, table, and chairs. It looked inviting, the table set for two people, with a low-hanging light fixture now turned to dim and candles down the center waiting to be lit.

On a cocktail table in front of the couch, a plate of appetizers was set out, along with a bottle of wine and two glasses, waiting for them. Soft music was playing. It was a scene set for seduction.

"Your apartment is beautiful." She walked over to the window. "And this view of the city is spectacular." Looking back over her shoulder, she asked, "Do you own anything without a great view of Philly?"

"Not if I can help it. Looking out at the city is one of the perks of urban life I wouldn't want to live without." He picked up the open bottle of wine and held it up. "Can I pour you a glass of wine?" She nodded and he poured two glasses. When he'd handed one to her, he raised his, touched it to her glass, and said, "*Salute. To us.*"

She took a sip then turned back to the window again.

In the reflection of the glass, she could see him watching her. "The view's not *that* riveting, is it *cara*?" he finally asked.

Without facing him she said, "I'm a little overwhelmed, I guess. This is the most perfect apartment I've ever been in." Now she turned to him. "The perfect apartment, drinking the perfect wine with the sexiest man in the city, which is a bit intimidating. Then realizing that you and my brother have the same taste in music for seduction, which is a little weird." She took another sip of wine before continuing. "I'm not sure what to say." She shrugged her shoulders to finish the sentence.

He tossed the pillows from the couch onto the floor, pushed a lampshade crooked, and threw a magazine onto a side chair.

"What are you doing?" she asked.

"Making the apartment a little less perfect for you, so you're comfortable."

"See, this is what I mean. You think a crooked lampshade is what less than perfect is."

"You mean it isn't?" He was mocking her, she knew.

"Of course it's not. You'd have to replace all the furniture in here as well as the artwork to make it less than perfect. And you know that. Not to mention you'd have to paint over the windows so you couldn't see the view."

"I'll mess up the living room and paint over the windows for you. I'll even run out and get cheap wine. But you just gave me a second compliment I'd like to keep. I've never been compared to Prince William and called the sexiest man in the city in one twenty-four hour period. I like it."

She laughed. "Enjoy the compliments if they mean so much to you. And please don't change the wine. It's delicious."

"So, paint the windows. Keep the wine. Enjoy the compliments. How about the music? Should I praise your brother's taste in music or change it because it feels weird?"

"The music is fine, and I'll pass along your admiration to my brother the next time I talk to him." She sipped at her wine again.

"I wasn't trying to make a statement with the music," he said. "And, to be honest, as much as I like them, I probably don't deserve the two compliments."

"I'm not sure you deserve them, either, now that I think about it. It was probably the wine talking."

"That's better. The Catherine Bennett I've gotten to know is reemerging from her slumber."

"Admit it. You set this scene so I'd be impressed."

"I'm happy that you like being here, but it's not a scene. It's home. I rarely invite anyone in except family. When I entertain, it's in restaurants. I protect this place like I do the roof garden. It's a place to relax, and this," the sweep of his arm took in the whole room, "this is comfortable for me, but I'd like you to feel at ease here, too."

She ignored the last comment, not sure it was a good idea to tell him how much she wanted to be comfortable in his apartment.

Not sure admitting it to herself was a good idea. "Did you do it yourself or have help?"

"It's all me. No consultants analyzed my color palette or feng shui-ed me, if that's what you mean."

"Not that there's anything wrong with consultants."

"Hell, no." He motioned her to join him on the couch. "I hope people don't ever start objecting to consultants. How else could I have bought this place if people objected to consultants?"

She laughed and nodded. "My point exactly." After she settled on the couch, he sat down close enough to her that she could smell whatever the scent was she'd been riding with in the elevator for months. She could feel the heat of him, she swore, even with the air conditioning running. To divert herself from thinking about either of those sensations, she said, "Dinner smells wonderful. It reminds me of my mother's cooking."

"I'm not surprised. We probably grew up with similar smells coming from the family kitchen. I made one of my mother's specialties—Bolognese sauce."

"My mother's is lasagna. I swear, no one in the world, even anyone in Italy, makes it better."

"You've been to Italy to compare?"

"No. I'd love to take Noah there some day, but it's never worked out. Have you been?"

"Several times. I still have distant relatives there."

"I imagine I do, too, although from the number of relatives I have here, it's hard to believe there are any left in the old country. The village couldn't have been that big."

As they continued to talk, Dominic took her hand, rubbing his thumb over the back of it. Halfway through her first glass of wine, she realized her shoulders had relaxed, her jaw had unclenched, and the frown lines between her eyes didn't feel so apparent. It was the wine, she was sure.

Right. It couldn't be the rhythmic stroking of her hand by the incredibly attractive man sitting opposite her. It couldn't be the clean, masculine smell of him or the warmth of his smile, the nearness of him. No, of course not. It had to be the wine.

"Catherine?"

It was obvious he had asked a question, but she had no idea what it was. "I'm sorry, I was woolgathering. What did you ask?"

An eyebrow went up, as did one corner of his mouth. "I don't usually lose a woman's attention for at least an hour. This time it took me only twenty minutes. I'm not sure if I'm getting better or getting worse." Before she could comment, he said, "Don't tell me. I'm not sure I want to know the answer. However, I would like to know if you'd like more wine."

"Thank you, but I think I'd better pass for now."

He poured himself a half-glass more. "Speaking of questions, you never answered mine."

"I thought you said you didn't want me to say if you're getting better or worse. I *was* paying attention to that."

"Not that one. The one about how you like to be seduced."

A surge of electricity went through her. Every cell in her body seemed on alert, waiting for what he would say—or do—next.

"I … um … I don't … didn't know how to answer. It's been so long since anyone has tried, I've forgotten, although the scene you've set—ah, your home—is pretty good."

"So, I've made the right start. Nice to know." He took the half-empty glass of wine from her hand and moved even closer, cupping his hand behind her neck, tangling his fingers in her hair. "Let's see what I remember from my research last night." He began to feather kisses from her temple down to her ear and neck. As he did, he pulled her closer to him. Her arms had a life of their own, it seemed, because without any thought on her part, they wrapped around his shoulders, pulling her body the rest of the way to his, until she was pressed against him and could feel his heart beating against her.

When he moved back to her mouth, the soft, feathery kisses turned hotter, deeper, more demanding. His tongue commanded hers; he nipped and sucked at her lower lip. She could barely breathe. The air in her lungs was gone; blood from her brain seemed to have disappeared, too. All she could feel was the need to have him touch her everywhere. His hands moved with assurance down her body as she arched toward him, and he responded by caressing the underside of her breasts. It was not enough to soothe the ache in them nor to satisfy the want in her body.

He broke from the kiss finally, as out of breath as she was. Touching his forehead to hers, he said, "You know I want you."

She nodded her head.

"Do you want me?"

"Yes, oh, God, yes."

He stood and pulled her up from the couch. She followed him, praying she knew where they were going.

Chapter 18

It had taken a will of impressive proportion, but Dominic had kept physical contact with Catherine to a minimum that afternoon. He knew that once he started he wouldn't want to stop. But making love in the middle of the roof garden wasn't what he had in mind for their first time, although the idea had merit for sometime in the future.

He'd been right to wait. The kiss in the living room just now proved it. After her response, her body molded to his, there was only one thing he wanted to do, one place he wanted to be. Where he'd wanted her to be for months—his bedroom.

The semi-sheer curtains over the window were already pulled so they wouldn't be awakened at sunrise the next morning. Now they served another purpose, creating an atmosphere of sensuousness as a filtered light played over the room. As dim as the light was, there was more than enough to see desire in the dark eyes Catherine raised to him when he took her in his arms. For a few moments, he stood with her in his embrace, inhaling the scent of her, sweet, tangy, and aroused, and enjoying the feel of her soft curves against him. But it wasn't enough. Nothing would be enough tonight except everything.

Holding her close with one arm, with his other hand he trailed his fingers down her throat to the first button on her silk shirt and popped it open. Then the second button. And the third. His fingers grazed the top of her breasts.

"Your skin is so soft. It's as silky as your shirt," he whispered into her ear before taking her ear lobe between his teeth and sucking gently.

"That feels good." Her arms tightened around him, and she pressed her body against his.

He finished unbuttoning her shirt and slipped it over her shoulders so it fell to the floor. "What else feels good? Does this?" He ducked his head and transferred his attention to a nipple, suckling it through a lacy, ice blue demi-bra. But it was still too much barrier for him and, from her response, for her. With a flick of his fingers, the bra was unhooked and on the floor with her shirt.

Saying, "I want to feel your skin against mine," she began to unbutton his shirt. She fumbled with the buttons but was taking too long for him, so he helped her finish the job and added his shirt to the growing pile of their clothes on the floor.

And then they were kissing again, her breasts tight against his bare chest, her fingers at the back of his neck, urging him with her mouth and her tongue to go on.

He whispered, "I need you naked. Now. First, this ..." He unbuttoned and unzipped her pants. They slithered down her hips and fell onto the floor. When she stepped out of them, he said, "Give me your foot, *cara*."

She raised one foot and he slipped off her stiletto.

"And the other."

Holding onto his arms to keep her balance, she obliged. When both shoes were off, she stood in front of him, her eyes downcast, suddenly seeming to be aware of how naked she was, clad in only a pair of light blue bikini panties. He took her hands when she tried to cover her breasts with her arms, saying, "You're even more beautiful than I imagined you'd be." He drank in the sight of her breasts with dusky pink nipples now peaked with desire, the flush of arousal on her olive skin. He wanted to be inside her, to hear her cry out his name as he made her his.

But he wasn't going to rush her. She may have been aroused by their kisses, but now, standing exposed in front of him, he could see from the nervous way she was glancing around the room and the rigid way she held her shoulders that she was more tense than aroused. So he slowed down, kissing her softly, nibbling at her mouth, skating his hands over the soft, soft skin on her back and hips, pulling her closer to him.

Breaking from the kiss, he guided her the two steps to his bed and lowered her onto it. He released her long enough to toe off his shoes, unbuckle his belt, unzip his pants, and in one motion, remove both pants and boxers. She averted her eyes as if to avoid looking at his body. When he joined her in bed, he could feel the tension in her arms and fisted hands. "Turn over, *cara*."

"Turn …? Why?"

He wasn't sure if she was curious or frightened. "I promised myself I'd touch every inch of your soft skin tonight. I want to start with your shoulders and back."

He didn't add that he wanted to massage away her anxiety so they could both enjoy what they were doing.

"Oh, I thought …" She didn't finish the sentence but obliged him and turned onto her stomach.

He began slowly, rubbing, massaging, then kissing her shoulders, moving down her spine to her hips and over her bottom. He could hear her breathing begin to hitch as he kneaded her tense muscles first into relaxation then arousal. He followed the massage with kisses along the backs of her legs to her knees. Then he went back to rubbing again, this time, the soles of her feet. Now fully aroused, she began to moan and move restlessly.

"Dominic, please, I want to see you; I want to kiss you."

"So you shall," he said as he helped her turn onto her back. He played with the lace at the edge of her panties, teasing, taunting until she raised her hips and pushed them down. He finished the job and pulled them off. Reaching for him, she brought his mouth to hers for an incendiary kiss. His legs tangled with hers, their bodies were as close as he could get them from shoulders to feet.

She was impatient in his arms, caressing his shoulders and back, her body pushing against his, one leg over his hip giving his now almost painful erection a cradle between her legs.

"Oh, God, Dominic. You feel so good."

"We haven't gotten anywhere near good yet, *cara*."

"Soon, please. Can we get there soon?"

"I'll do anything you ask me except that. There's no 'soon.' I intend to take my time, find out everything you like, enjoy how your body feels." He matched his words with his actions, surfing his hand over her from her breast to her hips and thighs. He didn't think he'd ever felt anything so soft, so smooth.

A moan was the only answer she gave, which he took as permission. He began another round of kissing, tasting his way from her mouth to her neck, to the pulse in her throat and then to her breasts where he lingered. With one hand, he lightly pinched a nipple into a peak while he did the same to the other nipple with his mouth.

As he moved from her breasts to her belly, circling her navel with his tongue, taking little love bites along the way, he felt her grind her hips against him. He thought she was close to orgasm, and he knew exactly how to take her over the top.

His kisses finally arrived at her sex, but as he settled himself between her legs, ready to finish what he'd started, she clenched her thighs together. When he looked at her, she was frowning slightly.

"Don't you like being kissed here?" he asked.

"I don't know. I've never …" She let the sentence die off, averting her eyes again. He had deduced from their earlier conversation she wasn't the most experienced woman he'd been with, but he was surprised at her awkward admission. He could feel the tension return to her body, when seconds before she'd been on the verge of coming apart in his arms.

"I'll stop then."

"No," she said after a moment's hesitation. "No, don't stop."

"Only if you promise you'll tell me if you don't like it." When she nodded, he began again, kissing from her breasts to her belly and then to her sex. This time, she didn't close her thighs, although he could still feel a slight tension in them. Gently, he pushed them further apart and touched her. She was so wet, so ready for him. The scent of her arousal was so sweet.

He looked up at her again and she nodded. He covered her with the flat of his tongue, tasting, licking, watching her for her reaction. When she canted her hips up, her eyes closed, her face softened with passion, he used his fingers to separate her labia and uncover her clitoris. With the tip of his tongue, he circled the already swollen bud, slowly at first then urgently. She was whimpering now, breathing his name over and over, clutching the sheets with both hands, moving against his mouth, reaching for release.

And when he inserted a finger into her now wet and ready channel, when he massaged inside her, she found it. With a cry, she climaxed.

• • •

Oh, my God. What had just happened? Sex had never been like this. It had always been arousing, and she'd usually had an orgasm, but this? His mouth, his hands, his body were beyond any experience she'd ever had. It was all so overpowering, so … there weren't any words she could come up with to describe it.

And he wasn't finished yet. There was the erection pressed against her hip still to be satisfied. But instead of pushing at her to take care of it, Dominic held her, stroking her back as she came down from the most amazing climax of her life. She felt dizzy, adrift in a place she'd never imagined existed, but safe and secure in his arms.

"Do you know how beautiful you are right now, *cara*?"

She didn't answer, couldn't answer.

With some concern in his voice he asked, "Catherine? Are you okay?"

"Not okay. It's the wrong word. There must be a better one. But I don't even know what it is."

He smiled against her face as he kissed her jawline on the way to her ear where he whispered, "Is it a good word, at least?"

"It would be the most amazing word I could think of, if I could think. You're the most amazing man. The most amazing lover." She sighed. "Tell me to stop before I say amazing again."

"I like the word." He pulled back and took her chin in his hand. "We're amazing together."

"I hardly think I had anything to do with it."

He took her hand and drew it down to his penis. "This is what you had to do with it. This is what you do to me. There's a connection between us, a chemistry, that's astonishing."

"Chemistry. Yes, we have chemistry. But it's because you're so …"

"No, it's because *we're* so … whatever it was you were about to say." He began to move her hand up and down on his member, and she felt the swirl of desire begin to build in her again.

"I don't think I've ever wanted anyone as much as I want you," she whispered.

"I don't have to *think* about it—I know I never have." He began again to caress her breasts and use his leg to part hers. Then he was crouched between her legs, holding her by the hips, pressing his erection against her sex, making her moan again with the need to feel him inside her. She was ready, wet and aching for him.

He pulled away. She made a small noise to protest, but when he grabbed a condom from the bedside table, she quieted.

"Here, *cara,* help me put this on." He handed it to her.

She fumbled with the packet, almost dropped the rubber when she got it out of the wrapper, but eventually, between the two of them, they sheathed him. Then slowly, very slowly, he entered her.

But she didn't want slow. She wanted all of him. She wrapped her legs around him and pulled him into her completely. It was the most wonderful feeling in the world. He filled her; all the empty spaces in her body were now full of only Dominic.

Slowly at first, then with increasing speed, he moved in and out, in and out, repositioning himself so he was rubbing his pubic bone against her clitoris, bringing her once again to the brink of climax and then, in one last thrust, bringing both of them over the top.

They lay together, arms and legs in a tangle with the sheets. The spicy smell she associated with him was now mixed with the mingled scent of sex and her perfume. Whatever she had thought being with Dominic would be like was a gross understatement of how good it had been. But she had no idea what to say to him or how to go on with their evening.

However, her stomach did. It grumbled and rumbled. Loudly. Dominic laughed. "So, you're hungry," he said, as he kissed her sweaty forehead.

"Apparently." She nestled into his chest. "But I don't want to leave here. It's so comfortable."

He drew back and smiled. "Ah, one more thing I won't do for you this evening. I won't serve you pasta Bolognese in my bed."

She pouted at him. "Why? I'm very neat. Remember? I didn't get one bit of the cioppino on my dress."

"That may be, but I'm not taking the chance." He tweaked her nose. "The sauce should be ready by now. Let's go cook pasta and make a salad."

"I guess this means I have to get dressed." She sat up on the edge of the bed and bent over to pick up her bikini panties.

"You can wear my shirt, if you'd like. I know I'd like. There's something very appealing about the idea of you wearing my shirt and that lacy bit of underwear while we sit in my perfectly ordinary dining room eating dinner."

"I'm not sure there's anything ordinary about you, Dominic, even your dining room." With one finger she lifted the shirt from the pile of clothes on the floor and swung it back and forth. "If I wear this, what will you wear?"

"I have other shirts, *cara*."

"Of course you do. How silly of me. I don't think you've worn the same suit twice in all the time I've been in the building. You must have an enormous closet to accommodate all the suits and shirts and ties and everything else. Exactly how large is it?"

"My closet? Why are you asking?"

"I want to see if I was right. I picture it being the size of one of the smaller states. Maybe sometime you'd let me look inside so I could count your suits." She was now in his shirt and her own underwear, wearing no shoes.

"You have interesting ideas of something fun to do. I'll try to remember it if I can't think of anything else to do with you in my bedroom. However, I doubt you'll have the chance to count suits any time soon." He'd pulled on his pants and grabbed a Polo shirt from a drawer. Taking her hand, he led her toward the kitchen. "If you can drag yourself away from contemplating my wardrobe, I think dinner's about ready."

Chapter 19

Although Dominic didn't usually want anyone around when he cooked, having Catherine in the kitchen with him seemed exactly right. As he finished up the sauce and put water on to boil for the pasta, she tore lettuce for the salad and diced fresh tomatoes he'd brought home from the rooftop garden. Together they added green onions, mushrooms, cucumbers, and black olives to the lettuce in a wooden salad bowl. Dominic mixed olive oil and balsamic vinegar and tossed the salad. Catherine sliced bread.

Working easily around each other, it was impossible for him not to touch her every chance he had—a caress on the back of her hand as he took a knife from her, a casual hip bump as they changed places around the cooking island, an accidental shoulder rub standing side-by-side tossing salad. She looked amused. He didn't care that she seemed to know exactly what he was doing.

When the pasta was cooked and the salad ready, they took it all to the table.

Dominic loved watching Catherine eat. She didn't pretend she didn't like food; she savored every bite. But then, she was raised in a good Italian family. And if the Alessandros were anything like the Russos, enjoying meals together was an integral part of being a family.

Even after they were ostensibly finished with their dinner, Catherine picked pieces of tomato from what was left in the salad bowl, finished the crusts of bread on her plate, took another forkful of the pasta from the serving bowl.

"I can send some of the pasta home with you in a take-out box, if you'd like," he said.

She blushed and put her fork down on her plate. "I'm not displaying very good table manners, am I? My mother taught me better, I swear. But it's so good I can't resist."

"I'm not complaining. I'm flattered."

"Do you cater? I can think of a whole lot of nights when having someone make this for Noah and me would be heaven."

"Maybe that's what I'll do when I retire—start a catering service for busy single moms. You'll be the first to know if I do." He reached across the table to her and took her hand. "But for the time being, let's go into the living room. I have a nice brandy there that'll settle our meal. Then we can think about dessert."

"You made dessert, too?"

"I thought we'd be dessert. Together. Assuming I can keep you in my bed and out of my closet."

• • •

The smell of coffee woke Catherine the next morning. She opened her eyes to a mug a few inches away from her nose held by Dominic, who was sitting on the side of the bed wrapped in a bath towel.

"Good morning," he said. "Do you usually sleep in this late on Sunday?"

"What time is it?"

"Nine thirty."

"You're joking. It's been years since I slept that late."

His smirk was back, but she didn't mind it so much this morning. "Must have tired you out last night."

"More likely it was the night before when I was up half the night wondering what you would say to me after the fiasco at the Academy."

"I like my version of it better." He held the mug of coffee just out of her reach.

"Is that for me?" she asked, licking her lips.

"It is after I get a kiss good morning."

"I need coffee right away in the morning or I'm not fit company." She grabbed the mug from him and emptied half of it in a few gulps. Then she placed it on the bedside table, put her arms around his neck, and kissed him. "Good morning, Dominic."

"Better." He ducked his head and gave her another quick kiss.

Slipping from his embrace she said, "It's so late, maybe I should take a quick shower and get out of your way."

The frown on his face made her unexpectedly happy. "Leave? I promised you breakfast. And Noah isn't home. What's the rush?"

"I don't want to overstay my welcome."

"That isn't possible, *cara*. Stay until you have to be home for him. I'd like to spend the day with you. Maybe have lunch at a little restaurant I know."

"Another one in Jersey?"

"No, this one is close to the old neighborhood where your mom lives. I bet you know it—Trattoria Tuscano."

"I do, but their Bolognese isn't as good as yours."

He laughed. "Thanks. But their *linguini con vongole* is better."

"If I keep eating meals with you, I'm going to have to rejoin the gym."

This time when he kissed her, his intent was much more serious. "I have a better way to work off the calories."

• • •

It was noon before they ate breakfast—or lunch—or brunch. Whatever the meal was called, it was delicious—fritattas with tomatoes, onions, and Parmesan cheese, fresh cantaloupe, and orange juice. They were lingering over coffee, and Catherine was on the verge of suggesting they clean up the dishes so she could go home, when Dominic sat up straight in his chair, leaned into the table, and said, "Could we break our 'no business rule' and talk business for just a few minutes?"

"Why not? We've broken it almost every time we've been together. What should we talk about this time?"

"Did you get the request for proposals from the Rittenauer Foundation?"

She was puzzled. That was not the subject she thought he'd raise. "A month or so ago. I think every communications firm in the city got the RFP. Why?"

"Are you going to submit a proposal?"

She sat back in her chair, ran her fingers through her hair, and sighed. "I wish. It's the biggest piece of work I've ever seen, and a five-year contract with them would be a huge break for my firm. But I don't have either the right staff or enough of the staff I do have to get the work done."

"You sub out your graphics work, don't you?"

Warily she said, "Yes. Usually. Why are you asking all these questions?"

Without answering her question, he asked another. "Have you ever jointly proposed on a big project with another communications firm?"

"No. We've included freelance copywriters or small graphics firms in a bunch of proposals but not with another firm like ours. What's this all about, Dominic?"

"It's about our two firms working together on a joint proposal for the Rittenauer Foundation work. Interested?"

"Jesus. Why?"

"Are you asking him or are you asking me?"

"I don't think Christ deals in petty things like joint RFPs. I'm asking you. Why would you even consider working with us when you've done work for the Foundation in the past and should have no trouble getting them to take you seriously?"

He paused for a moment, as if trying to decide if he'd continue, then said, "Not to compound my clichés but this requires a leap of faith here while I put all my cards on the table." After he resettled himself in the chair he began. "About a month before the RFP came out, I ran into Dick Rittenauer at an event. He was talking about what they were about to release. I was interested, of course. And he was excited. Said they were looking for a fresh approach to communicating with their publics, a rebranding, essentially. The board thinks they're perceived as out of touch, old-fashioned. He specifically mentioned the need for environmental and social considerations in everything they're doing, from the projects they fund to the way they run their business. He made it clear he didn't think the 'old established firms' would be able to come up with something that would, as he put it 'hit him between the eyes.' It was obvious he meant us."

"Oh. That's a bitch."

"It certainly is. So when I got the RFP, I debated about responding because I was afraid it was a waste of time. I put off making a decision until yesterday, when I went through it again. And I got thinking. What if the firm best known for socially responsible marketing teamed up with the firm with the deepest technical staff and proposed something to hit Mr. Rittenauer where he wants to be hit?" He sat back in his chair and watched her intently.

Catherine didn't know what to say. *He* had taken a leap of faith? Wasn't he asking her to take an even bigger one? Finally she said, "So, you get access to the brains and heart of my office and I get your graphics staff? Not sure that's exactly a fair trade."

He smiled. "I knew you'd come back with something like that. What I get is a chance—a chance, mind you—to win part of a huge contract because of your young, talented staff. What you get is financial management of the contract—which you don't like doing—a graphics staff, some pretty talented writers and editors even if they do work for me, and a group of people who know the Foundation like they know their own grandparents. I don't think either of us ends up with the fuzzy end of the lollypop."

Her mind was reeling, trying to sort out the offer, his reason for making it, what it meant for her and her company. Just thinking about it made her hyperventilate. "What does Edie think about this idea?"

"Haven't talked to her yet. Like I said, the idea just came to me yesterday. And I wanted to know if you were interested before I brought it up with her."

Catherine took a deep breath to get oxygen to her brain. "It's hard to get my head around the idea, and I can't give you an answer until I talk to my staff but …" She paused for a few moments before joining him in the leap. "Okay, I'll talk to them tomorrow."

"Good. I hoped you'd say that. I think we could do something very special together."

A terrible thought wormed its way to the forefront of her mind and made her frown. "I don't suppose there's any connection between …?" She waved her hand as if to include the dishes in front of them, the room, and everything else from the past twenty-four hours.

"Between making love with you and my idea about the Rittenauer proposal? What do you think?

"I'm not sure what to think. That's why I'm asking."

His laugh wasn't particularly humorous. "So, to your list of my lesser qualities—ruthless businessman, player, dastardly egomaniac, and smooth operator—I can now add prostitute as what you think of me?"

"Oh, dear God, is that what I just said?"

"Pretty damn close."

"I'm sorry. I didn't mean anything like that. My brain is just scrambled. First you blow me away with your lovemaking, then you hand me the chance to make my business almost as successful as yours. I'm not sure how to process it."

"I like the part about blowing you away with my lovemaking. In fact, I like that even better than the chance to pitch the Rittenauer

Foundation for a big contract. So, if I have to make a choice, I'll pick you in my bed. If you're concerned about my motives, don't take the idea any further. And if you ask your staff and they turn it down, it won't change my wanting you."

He reached across the table and took her hand. "I hesitated to ask you now because I was afraid you'd blend the two events together. The only reason I did was that when I was going through the RFP, it was obvious the clock's ticking. We've burned a lot of weeks doing nothing, and we need to get to work on it."

"When's it due? I don't remember."

"Right before Christmas. Whoever wins the contract is going to get one hell of a New Year's present."

• • •

Catherine got home just in time for her son to arrive back from his weekend with his dad. Noah politely introduced Dominic to his father and enthusiastically talked about the soccer game he'd played on Saturday. Everyone was cordial and pleasant, with Noah keeping the conversation going until Dominic and Andy left.

Which was a good thing because Catherine was still in a fog about the offer Dominic had made. She was sure her staff would jump at the chance to work with The Russo Group. She was tempted by the offer, of course, but worried that the way it had come about was questionable. Finally, she decided to take Dominic at his word and believe that his attention to her and the chance to work together weren't linked in any way.

She hoped.

On Monday, her intuition about her staff was confirmed. To say they were excited about working with The Russo Group would be to badly underestimate their eagerness. When Catherine asked who'd like to be on the team to develop ideas for the proposal, there were so many qualified volunteers she had a hard time selecting from among them.

She heard from Dominic it did not go so well in his office. Edie was adamantly opposed to the idea and put up a loud and long argument, saying they didn't need help coming up with as many good ideas as Bennett and Associates would. However, the rest of his staff agreed with Dominic. They were enthusiastic about working with the firm identified as innovators in their field. Edie eventually gave in to the pressure of the rest of the staff but turned down Dominic's offer for her to head up the Russo Group team. The rest of his staff fought to be on the project team, as Catherine's people had.

The die was cast. The Russo/Bennett team began to work on the proposal.

Chapter 20

Fall had arrived and with it cooler weather and the start of school and soccer for Noah. Because he was doing so well with the Kid-2-Kid program, Catherine lightened up on the rules enough for him to go to a Halloween party with his friends. Over the long Thanksgiving weekend, Dominic spent time with the Alessandro family, Catherine and Noah with the Russo family. It was getting more difficult with each passing week for Catherine to avoid facing Dominic's growing presence in her life. But what the relationship was, exactly, she couldn't say, although the enthusiastic acceptance from both their families of their being together, and the plans Dominic was making for them over the holiday season, would seem to indicate it was more than just casual dating. For the first time since her divorce, it appeared that Catherine had not only someone to accompany her to holiday events, but also a date for New Year's Eve. It was her favorite day in the holiday season, when anything seemed possible with the fresh start of a new year. And this New Year's Eve promised to be spectacular. Dominic had asked her to go with him to a black tie party at the new Barnes Foundation building on the Parkway.

Her fears that he was spending time with her for business reasons got lost in a flurry of dinners, social events, and the occasional weekend together throughout the fall. They were the talk of the building, according to Melody. Catherine asked Mel to keep the gossip to a dull roar, insisting it was still just a fling, even though neither she nor Dominic saw anyone else socially. In spite of his monogamous behavior, however, he never talked about how he felt. Not that she did, either, although she had a growing level of trust that he wouldn't do anything to hurt her.

To avoid trying to figure it out, Catherine did what she'd always done for distraction—she threw herself into her business, planning to worry about Dominic after the first of the year.

It wasn't hard to do. The Rittenauer Foundation proposal deadline was fast approaching, and the work was intense. The team from Bennett and Associates and the team from The Russo Group spent so much time together they were beginning to finish each other's sentences. No one had to ask what the daily coffee order would be. Everyone knew what every other person ate for lunch. Not to mention the details of their love life and the gossip from both offices.

The conference room on Catherine's floor where the team had set up headquarters was so messy, with the detritus of a dozen people almost living there, she was tempted to put a sign on the door warning it was a possible biohazard area. At their weekly staff meeting, she threatened to call in the EPA guys in the space suits to get it decontaminated unless the growing-ever-older-by-the-day pizza boxes and takeout containers were removed.

When the final draft of the proposal was ready, no one was happier to see the grins on the faces of the team that had put it together than the two principals. Catherine happily signed off on what she knew to be a brilliant piece of work, as did Dominic. On the Friday the proposal was due, Edie reviewed it, and took charge of having copies bound and messengered out to the Foundation headquarters in Haverford. Everyone on both teams was given time off until after Christmas, which was the following Tuesday.

To celebrate the successful work on the proposal as well as to enjoy the first weekend completely free of work since Thanksgiving, Dominic and Catherine planned an overnight in New York City. Dominic made reservations for a suite at The Plaza Hotel and bought theater tickets. Noah was with his dad. Everything was in place for a very special weekend.

It started by Dominic suggesting Catherine drive his Maserati. He said it was because he couldn't afford any more tickets, but from the look in his eyes, Catherine was sure it was because he wanted to give her the pleasure of driving his car. And pleasure was what she got as she sped along the Jersey Turnpike in a driving machine like no other she'd experienced.

Handing the car over to the valet parking attendant wasn't the easiest thing she'd ever done, but when Dominic promised she could drive them home, she relinquished the keys.

When they checked into their room, there was a chilled bottle of champagne waiting for them. "Did you do this or did the Plaza?" Catherine asked.

"I did. I thought we should start the celebrating right away," Dominic answered.

"Mister Russo, are you trying to get me intoxicated so you can have your way with me?"

"Actually, I thought I'd let you have your way with me today," he said. "So don't drink too much of this. I'm looking forward to it." He picked up the bottle. "Why don't you put your things in the bedroom while I do the honors?"

She hung up the dress she'd brought to wear to dinner and the theater and put her toiletries in the bathroom. Wanting to make sure things were okay in Philly, she checked her phone before going back to the living room. She had five messages, all from Melody, asking her to call immediately.

What the hell could be so important she'd call five times in less than an hour? The last time she'd had this many messages in such a short time Noah was in big trouble. *Please, God, not again.*

Cursing herself for turning off the phone while she drove up, Catherine called her office. Melody answered on the second ring. "Mel? What's going on? Is it Noah?"

"Noah's fine. Are you alone? Can you talk?"

"Alone? You know I'm with Dominic."

"Yes, but is he standing there? With you."

"No, he's in the other room. What the hell's going on?"

She could hear Melody take a deep breath and let it out slowly. "I called the Rittenauer Foundation to make sure the proposal got there. They said they had nothing from us."

"Maybe they didn't notice we're in with The Russo Group."

There was an ominous pause. "That's the thing. We're not."

"What do you mean, we're not? Of course we are."

"No, The Russo Group submitted a proposal under their name alone. We were cut out. Either they proposed their own ideas or …"

"Or stole ours and submitted them as theirs." Catherine's stomach took a nosedive. It couldn't be. He wouldn't. She tried hard not to believe it. "Are you sure?" Did you have them check a second time?"

"Yes, Catherine. I had them check every single copy of The Russo Group's proposal. Three times."

It *was* true. The man in the other room had totally and completely screwed her over. She'd been a fool to trust him. Of course he wasn't interested in her. He'd only been interested in what she could do for his business. And she'd gotten in so deep she could feel her heart cracking open.

"I probably should have waited until you got back but …" Melody began.

Catherine interrupted. "No, you shouldn't have. You did the right thing. I'll be back in Philly as soon as I can catch a train. I'll come directly to the office. Wait for me and get as many of the project team members as you can find to come in. This is about more than one proposal. I want to know exactly what was discussed about our business while they were working with that SOB's staff. We may have some serious damage control to do."

"I'm so, so sorry, Catherine."

"Yeah. So am I." She ended the call and stared at her phone for a few moments, feeling all the joy draining out of her life. Why hadn't she paid attention to her first instinct? She was a means to an end for him, nothing more. It should have been clear the day she moved into his building. The first thing he said to her was he wanted her to tell his staff what she did and how she did it. He wanted to suck her dry of information. Now he'd get a big contract because of her staff.

And if she was right and her people had shared a lot about their business during the time they were working together, he had an added bonus—he knew details about her business, how they operated, where her weaknesses were. He could continue to have an advantage over her. *Bastardo*.

Dominic appeared at the door of the bedroom, two flutes of wine in his hands. "You're taking a long time to unpack, *cara*. The bubbles in the champagne will be all gone if you don't get out here soon."

"Right. The bubbles in the champagne. With everything else under control, that's about all you have to worry about, isn't it?" She began to stuff her belongings back into her overnight bag.

"What do you mean?" He frowned. "And what are you doing?"

"What does it look like I'm doing? I'm packing."

"Is there an emergency? Is Noah okay?"

She went to the bathroom to get her toiletries. When she returned he asked again, "Catherine, I asked if there's something wrong with Noah."

"Noah's fine. My business, however, is not."

"Your business? What happened?"

She picked up her now repacked bag and started for the living room. "As if you don't know," she said, pushing past him.

"What do I know?" He followed her and put the glasses of wine on a table before blocking her access to the door of the suite. "Tell me. Just fucking talk to me."

"About what? How good you are at playing innocent? About how stupid I was to think you could actually be interested in me for myself? About how you betrayed me and screwed over my staff? There's nothing to talk about. I know what you did. I know why you wanted to get me out of town today. You can stop pretending." Her voice cracked, and she knew she had to get out of the room before she started crying. "Get the hell out of my way and let me go."

"Not until you tell me what's going on." His arms were crossed over his chest, his voice hard and angry.

"What's going on is you're a liar and a cheat and a goddamn son of a bitch who I never want to see again."

"I have no idea what brought this on. All I can see is you're angry without making any sense about why."

"I'm not making any sense? Right. Well, maybe this will." She grabbed one of the champagne glasses from the table and, saying, "Here. Do you understand this?" tossed the wine in his face, hitting him in the eyes. Then she threw the glass against the wall. "*Vai all'inferno*, Russo."

Taking advantage of his spluttering need to wipe wine from his eyes, Catherine ran out the door and down the hall. Conveniently, an elevator car was there, and she got to the lobby in seconds. Once outside the hotel, she grabbed a taxi and, as the cabby pulled away from the curb, watched out the rear window as Dominic roared out the door of The Plaza and looked up and down the street.

She ducked down and hoped he didn't see her.

Chapter 21

Dominic got pulled over for the first time less than ten miles into his drive on the Jersey Turnpike and was cited for talking on his cell phone while going thirty miles an hour over the speed limit. He didn't argue. He thanked the state police officer, shoved the tickets into the glove box, and took off. About fifteen minutes later, the same cop, who had apparently followed him, nailed him for the same two offenses. Dominic tried to explain this time but to no avail.

It was turning into a very expensive day. Four, hefty moving violations. A probable increase—again—in his car insurance. A hotel bill for a room he wouldn't be using. Theater tickets he'd given as a tip to the bellman for a play he'd never see.

Worst of all, for reasons he didn't understand, the day had cost him the woman he loved. He had to find out what the hell had happened and make it right. If he didn't, everything he'd planned for them for the weekend and for the New Year would be ruined, maybe forever.

Desperate to talk to someone who could help him find out what was going on, he'd first called his office, the cause of one half of his first set of tickets. The obvious thing connected to him that could make her so angry was the Rittenauer project, and he wanted to talk to one of his project team to see what they might know. Of course, none of the team members was there to help him out—he'd forgotten they were gone until after the holiday. When he asked to talk to Edie, oddly enough, she wasn't there either. No one knew why.

The second set of tickets came while he was talking to Catherine's office to see if he could get any help there. But none of her staff was available either. The Rittenauer team there was also off, and most everyone else had left early. He'd been pulled over before he could ask to talk to Melody.

Not wanting to risk a third set of tickets, he slowed down and didn't make another call until he stopped at a gas station. The third phone call was the charm. Dick Rittenauer gave him the answer he was looking for. It didn't take too many subtle—and not so subtle—questions to find out what had made Catherine go ballistic. Somehow, her firm had been cut out of the proposal The Russo Group had submitted to the Foundation. Dominic tried to explain there'd been a mix-up and he needed to amend the proposal, but he didn't make any headway. Telling Rittenauer he'd call again as soon as he returned to Philly, Dominic got back on the road. He didn't know how this had happened. He didn't know who had done it. But he sure as hell intended to find out, even if it meant he had to hunt down every last one of the project team at their homes over the weekend.

But first, he had to get Catherine to listen to him, to let her know he understood why she was angry, and to assure her he'd take care of it. And the only way he could think to do that was to get to her office before she went into hiding behind her staff. It's what he'd do if he were in her place, so he was guessing she would, too.

•••

Catherine burst through the doors to her office suite, the anger she'd been stoking since New York now at levels rarely seen outside steam turbines. "Melody, did you get hold of everyone on the Rittenauer team? Are they here?"

"Most of them, but ..."

Catherine stalked down the hall toward her office. "Get them all in the conference room. Right now. And get the coffee shop to send up two big carafes of coffee."

"Catherine, maybe you …"

She whirled to face her friend. "I don't want to hear 'maybe.' I want to hear 'sure, Catherine.' 'Whatever you want, Catherine.' 'Right away, Catherine.' Got it? Thanks to that son-of-a-bitch …"

"The son-of-a-bitch who's in your office at the moment."

"What the fuck? Why the hell didn't you tell me?"

Melody rolled her eyes but got serious quickly when Catherine glared at her. "He's been waiting for a while. I couldn't get him to leave. Maybe you should go back and see him."

"No, *we'll* go back and see him. If I see him alone, I'll kill him." Without waiting for an answer, she grabbed Melody's arm and dragged her down the hall.

Dominic struggled up from the couch when they entered, knocking his knee against the glass coffee table, muttering some curse word under his breath. "Catherine, you're here."

"Where the fuck do you think I'd be? I have damage control to do to save my business, you *figlio di puttana.*"

He recoiled, as if her words had pushed him back. But his voice was calm as he said, "Look, I found out from Dick Rittenauer what happened, and you have every right to be angry but …"

"Oh, how very kind of you to give me the right to be pissed off because you and your staff screwed us over."

"I had nothing to do with it. And I promise I'll get to the bottom of who did."

"Yeah, right. You really got your money's worth out of what you spent on me, didn't you, Russo? Not only the Rittenauer project, but also a way to damage my business in the future. Or was that just a happy coincidence?"

"I didn't … what do you mean, damage your business? How?"

"I'm on my way to talk to all the people your staff sucked information out of about my firm. Information you could use to wreck me."

"Why would I want to wreck you? And didn't your staff find out information about my business?"

"How could anything they find out crush the mighty Dominic Russo? You're the steamroller here."

He pulled at his hair, looking exasperated but still sounding calm. "Okay, let's leave all that for the moment. We can sort it out later. The important thing here is what happened. It has to be some huge mistake. You and I signed off on the same proposal. The exact one our teams put together. I don't know what changed between the time we signed off on it and the time it went out to Haverford."

She couldn't control the sneer. "Do you really think I'll believe that bullshit, Mister Not-One-Word-Goes-Out-Of-My-Office-Without-My-Knowledge-Because-My-Name's-On-The-Door?"

She had apparently struck a nerve because he lost the cool demeanor and started pacing. "For God's sake, Catherine, can't you trust me enough to believe I don't have any idea how this happened?" When he walked in front of her he reached for her hand, but she brushed him off.

"Trust you? *Trust* you? I trusted you with everything of importance to me—my son, my business. With me ... with my ... with everything, and you betrayed me."

"How do I convince you I didn't? Tell me. Whatever it is, I'll do it."

"There's nothing you can do to prove a negative. Even your powers of persuasion can only go so far. They don't cover this kind of deceit." She hitched her chin toward the office door. "Out. Now. And don't come back. I don't want to see you again."

"No, I'm staying for as long as it takes to make you see ..."

"Melody, call security and tell them I have an intruder I want out of my office." She looked at Dominic, shut her eyes, and said, "That won't work. The intruder pays their salaries." Then an idea occurred. "I know. Call The Roundhouse. Ask for Sergeant Jenkins or Sergeant Brown. Tell whoever you get that Tony Alessandro's sister has an intruder in her office. Give them our address. Say he's probably not armed, but he's big and might be dangerous. We'll need at least a couple patrol cars with lights and sirens outside the building."

Dominic glared at her. "You wouldn't."

"Watch me." She stood with her fists clenched, her arms crossed, and her eyes as cold as she could make them.

He threw up his hands in defeat. "All right. I'm leaving. But I'll get to the bottom of this. This isn't over, Catherine, not by a long shot. *We* are not over."

She waited until he left her office before she sank into her desk chair and covered her face with her hands.

Melody touched Catherine's shoulder. "I'm so sorry, Catherine. You were right not to get serious with him."

Catherine raised her head from her hands and looked at her friend. She let the truth show on her face for the first time.

"Oh, my God. You're in love with him, aren't you?"

"Damn it." She felt the tears begin to fall. "I should've listened to you. But I didn't. I was stupid."

Melody was silent for a while, comforting her friend with soothing sounds and soft strokes on her back. Finally she said, "Look, I'm pretty good at reading people, and he sure didn't act guilty to me. Maybe you're jumping to conclusions. Maybe …"

"Maybe you're a victim of Mister Sex on Legs, too, Mel. Don't fall for it. He can't be trusted. He brags about how persuasive he is. That doesn't mean he's telling the truth when he's being persuasive."

Melody shrugged. "You know him better than I do, I'm just saying …"

Catherine wiped her eyes and got up from her chair. "What I'm saying is let's go talk to the Rittenauer team and see what the damage is. Then I think I'm going to go home until after Christmas."

"Which, since it's on Tuesday, isn't a whole hell of a lot of time off. Maybe you should think about taking it easy while Noah's in Oregon with his uncle and come back to the office after New Year's."

•••

Once in his office, Dominic found out what had happened. She hadn't even bothered to hide her tracks. In less than ten minutes, the IT guy pulled up the files Edie Martin had amended, removing all mention of Bennett and Associates from the proposal, rewriting parts of it so all the work was done by The Russo Group. If it hadn't been so terrible a thing to do, Dominic would have been impressed with how easily and quickly she had made the changes.

He tracked Edie down at home and asked her to come to the office.

Expecting an ugly scene, he asked his HR manager and his IT expert to join him in the conference room. He'd have had the lawyers there, but they'd closed for the holidays already.

Edie seemed to think, from the smug and self-satisfied look on her face, she'd been called in to be praised.

"Edie, I found out what you did to the Rittenauer proposal. We made a deal with Bennett and Associates to propose jointly and you ..."

"And I saved us from making a huge mistake. You said we should keep an eye on our competitors, and I did. I have no idea how she seduced you into making the deal, but I got you out of it. It would give credibility to her and her band of hipsters to be working officially with us. I expect you'll be giving me a raise for it."

She seemed genuinely puzzled when he replied, "A raise? For lying? Cheating colleagues? I don't do business like that and you know it. You've been here long enough to know …"

"Long enough to know you have a weakness for pretty faces. You don't ever look for a woman who's solid and loyal. Someone who's done nothing but help you for years. No, you go after the newest bright, shiny thing. I've seen it happen time after time."

Jesus, Catherine was right. Edie was possessive of him. She was jealous of Catherine. That's why she did this.

"Whatever you believe about me personally," Dominic said, "I won't have the firm's reputation destroyed by what you did yesterday. You have fifteen minutes to pack up your desk. Your services are no longer needed here."

"You're firing me? You can't do that. Not after what I've given to you, to this firm. You can't survive without me."

"I can and I will. Security is waiting to escort you from the building."

"You'll regret this. I'll sue you," she yelled as the HR manager led her to the door of the conference room. "That bitch has you mesmerized. But you'll see. She's no different than all the others. You'll get tired of her."

When he was sure she was gone, Dominic went back to his desk and slumped into his chair. What a mess. If he didn't get it straightened out quickly, both his personal and professional lives would be in the dumpster. He could rebuild the reputation of his business over time, but he'd never be able to replace the woman he'd been about to ask to marry him.

There was only one place to start. If Catherine wouldn't listen to his words, he had to convince her with his actions. He grabbed for the phone and punched in a number.

Chapter 22

After she met with her staff, Catherine went home. It was safer there than in a building where she was bound to run into Dominic, so she planned to work from home for a while until she figured out how to deal with him and the fallout from the Rittenauer debacle. When Melody called a day later, she said she was working on a plan. When Noah asked if he would see Dominic before he left for Oregon, she said he was booked with family obligations. She lied to her mom and said he couldn't make Christmas Eve because he was out of town. She wasn't sure any of them believed her, but it was the best she could come up with.

The truth was, she didn't know what the next step was. She knew she had to at least apologize for her fit of temper with the champagne in New York. And for sticking him with a hotel bill for a suite they hadn't used. Oh, and for the scene in her office. She should probably apologize for threatening him with the police. Maybe for not listening to his explanation, although she was still sure she'd been justified there.

Every time she thought about it, her embarrassment got deeper. Her behavior was not what one expected of a successful businesswoman but more like that of a three-year-old, if three-year-olds threw champagne and threatened their lovers with the cops.

She survived, if not enjoyed, Christmas Eve and Christmas dinner with her family. As she drove home from getting Noah on the plane for his trip to see his Uncle Tony in Oregon, she made a promise to herself—she'd figure this out by New Year's and get on with her life. She'd been just fine before Dominic Russo, and she'd be just fine without him. Wouldn't she?

• • •

A week later, Catherine had not kept her promise to herself. She still hadn't put in an appearance in her office, and she was starting to feel silly about hiding like a coward in her townhouse. Even if she felt justified in her anger, she'd behaved badly with Dominic and had to face the consequences—how many times had she told her son that recently? Not that she had much of a plan of action. All she had was the same to-do list she'd started the week with: apologize to Dominic for her immature behavior. Tell Noah and her family Dominic was out of the picture in her personal life. Figure out how to deal with him on a professional level. Pick up the pieces at work and return to her usual routine.

Jesus. This was not how she planned to start the New Year. This was to be the year her favorite time of the season was going to live up to her fantasies. She was going to spend New Year's Eve with a handsome and charming man at a party that was bound to be something out of a movie. At midnight he would kiss her tenderly, maybe even tell her he loved her. There would be champagne and balloons. It would be a perfect beginning to what she had hoped would be a fresh start in her life with the New Year.

Sadly, the operative words in that sentence were "had hoped." Because all her plans and dreams had all gone to hell with the Rittenauer project debacle.

Catherine still didn't know how to deal with what Dominic had done. If he'd been anyone else in the city, she could just ignore him for the rest of her life and talk about him behind his back. But he was her landlord, she saw him almost every day in the building, and he was in the same business. In their small community, trash-talking him would, she was afraid, only get her a black eye and wouldn't do him any harm.

In one half-serious moment she thought about sending him flowers. There was a certain symmetry to the idea. It was how their relationship had started, after all. Perhaps it was the way it should end. All she had to do was find flowers that said, "I'm sorry for throwing wine at you," "I'm furious for what you did," and "Here's to the end of a relationship."

She hadn't heard from him since right before Christmas. No surprise. She'd ignored the attempts he'd made to contact her. And there was the little matter of telling him she never wanted to see him again when he'd been in her office. She'd paid no attention to his messages. He'd obviously gotten hers.

If she didn't hear *from* him, she heard *about* him. Melody relayed all the gossip buzzing around the building. Catherine pretended it didn't matter, although privately she was as fascinated by the contradictory rumors as Mel was.

And the rumors were wild. Edie Martin hadn't been seen around the building since right before Christmas, but no one knew why. Was she on vacation? Was she so outraged by what had happened with the Rittenauer proposal she'd quit? Or was she responsible for what had happened and been fired? Then there were the rumors about the proposal. The Rittenauer Foundation had awarded The Russo Group the contract. The Russo Group had lost to an out-of-town firm. The contract had been signed. Oops, no, there was some hitch in the negotiations. It seemed like there was something new every day.

Catherine knew it was driving Mel crazy. Her friend couldn't nail anything down, because her best source in Dominic's office wouldn't talk, no matter how hard Mel tried to pry the news out of her. All she had to go on was what the barista told her, and who knew where he got his information.

Then, the day before New Year's Eve, Melody called. Her source had talked and she had hot news.

She started with, "I have some good news, some bad news, and some good news. Also some 'I'm not sure what it means' news. Which do you want first?"

"I can't begin to make sense out of that list. Just tell me what you know, please."

"Well, first, Edie Martin was fired from The Russo Group. It's definite. Dominic had her escorted from the building the day you came back from New York."

"You're joking. How come you didn't know for sure before now?"

"Everyone in The Russo Group was asked to keep things quiet until Dominic could sort out what happened."

"What does that mean?"

"That's the part I can't figure out. It's apparently no secret within his company that Edie was the one who switched the proposals. No one else knew anything about it. But they were sworn to secrecy until today, when it suddenly became okay to talk about her being fired."

"Edie did it? Oh, shit."

"I thought you might react that way."

"But why is everyone talking now?"

"That's the part I can't figure out," Melody admitted. "Seems to me they should be keeping it all under wraps. She could have wrecked The Russo Group's rep with her stunt. But now it's okay to talk about her being fired, but there's something else going on that no one can talk about."

"Are you sure about all this?"

"Absolutely. Impeccable sources. So, just to recap: Good news—Edie was the culprit. Bad news—you blamed the wrong person. Good news—Edie was immediately fired. Not-sure-what-it-is news—there's something else brewing up on the fifteenth floor."

When Catherine didn't immediately respond, Melody asked, "Are you still there?"

"Sorry, yeah, I'm still here. Just trying to process what you said."

"So, what're you going to do?"

"Hell if I know. This just complicates things. At least before I knew it was all Edie's fault, I could cling to a small vestige of justification for my behavior. Now …"

"Now you have to apologize big time."

"Yeah, right. Groveling to Dominic is not exactly how I wanted to start the New Year."

"No, I'm pretty sure you wanted to start the New Year doing something else with Mister Sex on Legs. Unless he's into the whole dom/sub thing and you haven't told me about it."

"Not now, Melody. I'm not in the mood."

"Okay, I'll leave you alone. When will you be back in the office?"

"January second. Bright and early. Eating humble pie all the way from the lobby to the fifteenth floor, it looks like."

"See you then. I'd say Happy New Year, but I have a feeling you'd yell at me."

• • •

New Year's Eve might not be turning out the way she wanted it to, but the least she could do was greet the New Year with a tidy house. Her bedroom and the living room were adorned with discarded, mostly unread, newspapers and books from her week of failing to distract herself with escape reading. Empty take-out containers and dirty dishes decorated the kitchen because she'd been too unmotivated either to cook or clean up. A sad-looking Christmas tree was dropping needles all over the floor of the dining room because she'd forgotten to give it water. For a woman who hated clutter, she'd certainly managed to live in it since she'd holed up in her house.

So, she decided to clear things away, take a shower, and get into clean clothes. Maybe, she thought, she'd even cook something for dinner and watch New Year's Eve in Times Square. A million people eager for the New Year to arrive might convince her to feel the same.

Some of the plan worked. By eight everything was tidy, she was showered and in her favorite yoga pants and tank top. She plugged in the lights on the Christmas tree, flipped on the gas fire, and put on some background music. The idea of cooking had lost its appeal, however, so she ordered a pizza. Less than ten minutes after she called, there was a knock on the door. She scrambled for her purse and opened the door saying, "Wow, that was …"

But it was no pizza delivery guy standing on her doorstep in the lightly falling snow. It was Dominic wearing a tux, a white silky-looking scarf, a black coat, and a wary expression.

"Oh … uh … hello." Avoiding his eyes, she tried to find someplace where it was safe to rest her gaze. But there wasn't one place on his whole freaking body that didn't send her hormones into high gear just from looking at him. Damn him. "What're you doing here?"

"I came by to wish you Happy New Year, Catherine, and talk to you about something." He held up a bottle. "I brought champagne. I hoped this time you'd drink it with me instead of throwing it at me."

She winced, embarrassed at the memory of what had not been her finest hour. "I owe you an apology for that. I don't know what happened. I've never done anything like it before."

"You were angry, quite rightfully, given what you'd just found out. Although I would have preferred conversation to dramatic gestures." He brushed snow off one coat sleeve. "May I come in? It's a little wet and cold out here."

She reached up to help him de-ice himself but regretted it as soon as her hand touched his shoulder. Even through his cashmere coat and tux, she felt the tingle that always hit her when she was around him. Now she was the one who was shivering, and it wasn't because she was inappropriately dressed for the cold air streaming into her house.

Looking around him at the Escalade parked at the curb, she asked, "Is Jack sitting out there? Shouldn't you ask him in out of the cold, too?" *Please ask him in. I need a chaperone, a barrier, someone to keep the conversation on safe topics until I can pull myself together.*

"Jack's off. I drove myself." He stepped into her entryway, glancing up and down her body. "Doesn't look like you have plans for the evening."

"Ryan Seacrest can't see me from Times Square, so I decided to be comfortable. You look like you're on the way to the party at the Barnes Foundation." She headed for the kitchen and he followed.

"No, I'm dressed like this because I'm reduced to using my wardrobe to get your attention. You once said you liked the way I looked in a tux, so I thought I'd wear it in the hope it would soften you up enough to get me through the door. It seemed a better option than more roses, although I was tempted."

He draped his coat and scarf over a chair and waited for a few moments, holding the bottle out to her with an inquiring look. When she didn't move to retrieve glasses for the champagne, he shook his head and got them.

He poured two glasses of wine and handed one to her. "Happy New Year, Catherine." He touched his glass to hers.

She started to raise her glass then put it down on the counter. "I can't do this, Dominic. I can't pretend we're just celebrating New Year's like nothing's happened."

"I'm not suggesting …"

"Please, let me get this out." She finally raised her eyes to him. "I owe you an apology. Actually, a lot of apologies. Enough that I don't know where to start. At the same time, I'm so damn mad at you it makes me crazy. And I'm even madder at myself for being mad at you because I guess you didn't have anything to do with what happened, but I don't care, I'm still mad."

"Sounds complicated. How about we make it simple and issue blanket apologies to each other and go on from there?"

"Apologies to each other? Why would you apologize to me?"

"Because you were right about Edie and I brushed it off. She *was* possessive. She was jealous of you, and that's why she did what she did to the proposal. I should have seen it. I didn't. And I'm sorry."

"That hardly compares to throwing wine at you, threatening you with the police, saying mean things to you, ignoring all your attempts to talk to me."

"I didn't like the face full of champagne more because it was a waste of expensive wine than any other reason. And it was worth being threatened with the cops to see the expression on your face. You do fierce very well. The rest ..." With a wave of his hand, he dismissed her ranting and deleting his emails, texts, and phone calls without reading or responding to them. "If I'd paid any attention to the signals Edie was giving out every time she was around you, I could have headed off the whole thing. I didn't. So, that's my apology." He lifted his glass to her. "Now, it's your turn."

"Is it really that easy?"

He nodded. "It is as far as I'm concerned."

"Okay, if it is, I apologize, too. For the champagne, threatening you with the cops, throwing you out of my office, ignoring your calls. Please forgive me."

"Good. That's out of the way. Now, about the part where you're still mad. I have something that may make a difference." He set his glass on the counter, pulled a folded eight-and-a-half-by-eleven manila envelope from the inner pocket of his overcoat and handed it to her. "When I couldn't get your attention with words, I decided I'd stop trying until I could prove to you with action that I meant what I said about setting things straight."

"Action? What do you mean? What is this?" She tried not to look curious although she was.

"It's three copies of a contract I signed this afternoon. Dick Rittenauer signed them yesterday, and you need to sign tonight or tomorrow."

"Contracts? For what?"

"For the Rittenauer Foundation work, of course. I convinced Dick to look at the real proposal, the one you and I signed off on before Edie changed it. When he realized most of what he'd been impressed with came from your shop, he asked his board to amend the contract they'd offered me. It took a while to get them all together because of the holiday, but when he finally did, they agreed. The contract you're holding reflects what our two firms developed together." He shrugged, a half-smile on his face. "Well, it's not quite what we signed off on. Dick thought your firm should have more of the budget. He changed it so you do."

She still hadn't opened the envelope, stunned by his words. Finally, and very quietly, she said, "This is an incredibly generous gesture. I don't know what to say."

"There's nothing to say, other than 'where do I sign?' And it's neither generous nor a gesture. It's making it right. I can't have the good reputation I've carefully cultivated for years damaged by a vindictive woman. And I won't let your staff get cheated out of the work they developed. Most importantly, I couldn't disappoint a client. They should get what they contracted for."

She could feel herself tearing up and tried to wipe her eyes without him seeing her. Of course he did. With what seemed like great caution, he moved the two champagne glasses out of her reach before extending his hands to her. She couldn't help smiling. "I promise I won't throw any more champagne."

"I'm relieved. But why are you crying? I thought you'd be happy, not sad." He took her hands and tried to draw her closer. She resisted.

"I *am* happy."

"Then come here and tell me how wonderful it will be to work together."

"Maybe I … it's just that … I still feel like I owe you a big *I'm sorry.*"

"I thought we were past that."

"It doesn't feel that way to me." She took a deep breath. "There's more I regret. There's … well, everything else."

"Everything? How far back are we going here?" He had an all-too-familiar wry smile on his face.

"New York. Just to New York."

"Thank God. I was worried you were going to say you're sorry you wasted your time with me. Which would make me worry about losing my touch …"

"I'm trying to seriously apologize here, Dominic."

"You already did. Look, you had a reason to be angry when Mel told you what happened. And as much as I don't like being lumped in with your ex-husband, I even understand a little why you might think I'd do something like that. It had happened before—a man you trusted betrayed you. I'd hoped you'd learned to trust me, that I'd earned your trust."

"You did. I had. At least, I thought I had. When Melody called me yesterday and told me the whole story, I had to finally admit to myself I should have known you wouldn't … you didn't … do what I accused you of. But it got all mixed up with being pissed off that you got the work my people had developed. I knew I had to apologize, but I was still seething about our work being stolen. So I took the coward's way out and avoided you."

He grinned as he returned her to his embrace. "Well, then, aren't we lucky I don't give up when I'm after something I want?"

"You have told me that once or twice."

"Yes, I have. And what I want is you. Always have. I love you. You have to promise, however, in the future you'll let me explain things before you waste really good champagne." He kissed her forehead. "Which reminds me—you owe The Plaza for a broken glass. I paid for the room but told them to bill you for the glass."

"You love me?" She kept her face hidden in his shirt so he couldn't see the hopeful expression she knew was on her face.

"Yes, Catherine. I love you." He lifted her chin with his forefinger and gently touched her mouth with his. "I believe this is the place where you say, 'I love you, too, Dominic.'"

She laughed. "I love you, too, Dominic."

"Maybe the next time you can say that without prompting, but it'll do for now." He ducked his head to kiss her again, but just before his mouth met hers, seemed to reconsider. "Hmm. This might be a good place to give you your Christmas—well, New Year's now, I guess—present."

"Oh, I have one for you, too. I'll go get it." She started to pull away from him but he stopped her.

"Let me give you yours first." He reached into the pocket of his jacket and brought out a small box. It was a distinctive blue and had a red ribbon around it. He handed it to her saying, "Happy New Year, Catherine."

She stared at the box for a long moment. "I thought Tiffany used white ribbon."

"That's your reaction? You object to the color of the ribbon?" He was smiling as he said it.

"No, no, I'm not objecting. I was just surprised." She couldn't bring herself to open the gift, afraid to hope she knew what was inside.

"At Christmas, I was told when I asked, they use red ribbon." He pulled on the end of the bow and the ribbon fell away. "Now, you open it the rest of the way."

Inside was a diamond ring in a classic Tiffany setting. "It's beautiful," Catherine said, trying hard not to cry.

"No, *cara*, you're beautiful. The ring is only a reflection of that."

She removed the ring from the box and started to put it on.

"Let me," he said and slipped it on the ring finger of her left hand. "Marry me, Catherine. I don't want to spend another New Year's Eve wondering if you'll be with me at midnight."

She didn't answer but only shook her head. "This sure makes the cashmere sweater I got for you look insignificant."

When he could stop laughing he said, "Tell you what, wrap that sweater around a 'yes, I'll marry you,' and we'll call it even."

She put her arms around his neck and kissed him lightly. "You have yourself a permanent New Year's Eve date, Mr. Russo. I'd love to marry you."

"Good. Now, how about we continue this conversation …"

Whatever he was going to suggest was interrupted by the doorbell. "You're expecting someone else? I thought you said your date was the guy on television," he said.

"It's my pizza." She broke from his embrace, grabbed her purse, and went to the door. When she returned, he had removed his jacket and bowtie, undone a couple studs in his shirt, and brought down two dinner plates from the cabinet.

He took the box from her and opened it. "Anchovies and olives? Interesting choices." Popping an olive into his mouth, he added, "I've never started a New Year with pizza and Dom Perignon. If we like it, we may have to make it a tradition. But we seem to be missing dessert." His smile was sinful.

Catherine tried to keep from matching his expression as she picked up one of the plates. "Oh, I'm sure we can rustle up something. Maybe something Italian, like tiramisu. What do you think?"

"I think life's short and we should have dessert first." He took the plate from her hand and set it down on the counter. "How do you feel about cold pizza?"

More from This Author
(From *Lights, Latkes, and Love* by Peggy Bird)

"I *hate* the public. Hate, hate, hate the public." Hannah Jenkins spit out the words as she flopped into an overstuffed chair and waved away the glass of wine her housemate Sarah offered.

"Really? The entire public? Worldwide? Or just Portland, Oregon, and its environs?" Sarah accompanied her question with an exaggerated eye roll.

"Okay, maybe not *all* the public. Just the ones who're a pain in the butt this time of year. Which, face it, is a large number."

"Sure you won't have a glass of wine? It might take the edge off your pissed-offness."

"If I start drinking tonight, I might never stop until the damn Christmas season is over. Which is weeks away. By then, I'd do in my liver and my tombstone would read, 'She was right: Christmas killed her.'"

Hannah was the manager of the flagship—and largest—store in a chain of women's specialty shops. She'd worked her way up from part-time clerk to sales associate to buyer and now to store manager, all by the age of thirty-two, an impressive accomplishment. She loved working in the heart of the city. Loved her colleagues. Loved everything about working retail.

Except Christmas. She hated Christmas.

Sarah settled on the couch and took a sip of her wine. "Maybe if you vent, you'll be in a better mood for the dinner I've spent the last hour preparing. So, tell me, what happened today?"

Hannah knew her housemate was asking only because she was a good friend. Sarah had heard this particular rant each year at this time ever since they'd moved in together.

"Not everyone was an asshat," Hannah admitted, "but there were enough to prove that the idea that everyone has a generous holiday spirit is a huge lie."

"Specifics, please," Sarah said with an annoying grin. "You know me. I don't like generalities."

"Okay, there was this jerk who spent a boatload of money on a miniscule bit of lace the manufacturer calls a 'nightgown.' For his girlfriend, he said."

"What's so bad about that?"

Hannah snorted. "He also bought a pair of bunny slippers and a flannel nightgown for his wife and a second nightgown for his secretary—who, I'm sure, does more than print out his schedule for him."

"Oh."

Hannah was almost happy to see her housemate's disappointed slouch. "After him was the woman who thought she could bargain with me for the last bottle of 'Tragic' perfume in the entire city. Telling me that since it was the last one, we couldn't advertise it, so I might as well let her take it off my hands. Like I'm gonna give her a break on the price of the hottest scent to come along since Chanel No. 5. She was so pissed off she filled out an official complaint form saying I wasn't living up to the store's customer-friendly reputation." By now Hannah was sitting with her spine in military alignment, her chin jutting out and her hands in fists.

"But the topper was the woman who said her two teacup poodles were service dogs, so we couldn't ask her to leave them outside. She asked one of my sales staff to hold them while she tried on a half-dozen dresses. Said she was looking for something special for her Christmas-card picture. When she finally decided on one she liked, she grabbed the stupid dogs back to see how they looked with what she'd chosen, and one of the little furballs peed all over the five-hundred-dollar dress, which the woman then refused to buy."

"Don't get angry at the dog. It's not his ... her ... fault."

"I'll apologize to the dog if I ever see it again. But damn it—"

"I get it. Bad day at the office." Sarah waved her hand at the bottle on the table. "A bit of the grape might make you feel better about it. Are you sure you won't join me?"

"Maybe I will." Hannah pulled herself out of the depths of the chair and poured a small glass of wine. "I swear, if this job wasn't the best I've ever had, I'd quit. Or at least take a leave until January."

If she were honest about it, Hannah would have to admit she didn't hate everything about working retail during the holidays. For example, she loved the profits. And she didn't object to some of what went along with the season, like the background music that played endlessly from Thanksgiving through Christmas Eve. Didn't even mind having to put up the glittery decorations the night before Thanksgiving so the store was ready to greet shoppers on Black Friday.

It was what happened beginning on Black Friday that she hated—people showed up to shop. There was the crux of her problem. She was ashamed to admit to anyone except her roommate that nasty, stressed, badly behaving customers were the reason she'd come to hate the entire Christmas season. No one seemed to be happy this time of the year. At least not that she noticed. People came into her store, made demands, treated her staff badly, and killed any sense of joy by behaving like—well, like toddlers who hadn't napped in a week. Or kindergartners deprived of their afternoon snacks. Or infants who'd lost their pacifiers.

Sadly, those pathetic examples of Christmas cheer she'd just vented about to Sarah were only the tip of the iceberg. She hadn't even mentioned the shoplifters and credit-card scammers or the people who deliberately damaged merchandise to try and get a discount. Sure, they were around the rest of the year, but the holidays brought more of them out of the woodwork.

Hannah had tried to tell herself that, as manager, she only had to deal with the customers who were difficult, and didn't see the nice people who were there every day. Tried to believe that not everyone was a PITA. But the closer it got to Christmas, the more difficult it was to believe when all she ever saw was a long line of belligerent people like the teacup poodle woman. And all her staff gossiped about were people like the man who'd involved her store in his cheating ways.

If this was what the holiday spirit was about, she wanted none of it.

Which was sad because when she was younger, she'd loved Christmas—the food, the presents, the anticipation, the lights. She especially loved the lights. She'd grown up on Peacock Lane, a four-block-long street in southeast Portland known for its Christmas-light displays. Every house on the lane was a glowing celebration of the season. Trees, bushes, rooflines, doors— everything that could support lights was draped in them. When it was lit up for its annual celebration of the season, the street was visible from the international space station, her father used to tell her. She believed him until she was a lot older than she liked to admit.

Hannah couldn't pinpoint the exact moment her enjoyment of the season had begun to wane. It could have been the year her family's beautiful light display, along with several others on the street, was damaged by vandals, leaving her wondering why anyone would attack something her family and their neighbors did as a holiday present for strangers.

Maybe it was when one too many customers treated her badly on the sales floor, stressed out by the season, and disappointed not to find what they were looking for.

Or perhaps it was because her first serious relationship had fallen apart just in time for the holidays. When she was twenty-six and had been promoted to buyer, she'd gotten involved with the manager of a sister store in a large regional mall outside Portland. He was a bit older than she was and had surprised her with his interest. After only a few months, she had hopes that the relationship would turn into something serious in the New Year.

Then she discovered: (1) The man she thought was the love of her life had backstabbed her, blaming her selection of stock for his failure to reach his sales goals; (2) she was just the latest in a long line of buyers he'd romanced to get what he wanted for his store; and (3) he never, ever, kept a relationship going over the holidays, so he could be free to roam various boozy Christmas parties and take advantage of the ubiquitous mistletoe. He became, to her and to her friends, like Voldemort, he-whose-name-was-forbidden-to-be-spoken. She had vowed never again to get involved with a coworker. Running into the dipshit every few weeks had made recovering from the relationship difficult. It was only after he moved out of state that she could breathe easier during company-wide events.

Whatever the reason—a relationship gone bad, the dissatisfied customers, the ruined Christmas display—by the time she was promoted to store manager, she was fed up with Christmas, and not about to have her opinion challenged by anyone.

Between sips of wine, Hannah continued to vent to her housemate. "In addition to dealing with teacup poodles and philandering husbands, I got two new assignments today. Angie's pregnancy isn't going well, and she'll have to go on medical leave for the next few months until the baby arrives. So, on top of worrying about her and not having any luck filling the two weekend staff slots we have, now I have to organize the Christmas party Angie always worked on, too."

She sighed. "*And* Mr. Austin has decided to involve the entire chain in a huge Christmas deal for some charity. He's called a staff meeting for tomorrow before the store opens and I'll find out then what our store will be responsible for."

"Sorry to hear about Angie. I hope it works out okay. But I'm sure you can handle the extra work." Sarah raised her wineglass, but before she took another sip said, "You know, you could always convert. Being Jewish this time of year is kinda fun. I get to enjoy all the lights and songs without worrying about anything except eating too many latkes and gaining a couple pounds."

"What are you talking about? You have to buy presents for eight nights of celebrating."

"That's only if you have kids. The adults just have eight nights of good food and candle lighting. At least in my family that's how we do it."

Hannah cocked her head, a small smile appearing for the first time since she'd come home from work. "It has its appeal, believe me. Although changing religions wouldn't get me out from under the responsibility of planning the store's Christmas party. And it wouldn't make the crabby customers go away." She finished her glass of wine. "But thanks for listening. I feel better. Let me help you get dinner on the table."

"Nope. My night to cook and serve. Yours to clean up. Pour us each another glass of wine while I dish up. I made your favorite lasagna."

"The longer I live with you, the more I wonder why I'd ever want to consider marrying some guy who can't cook, doesn't pick up after himself, and never learned to do the laundry."

Sarah looked back over her shoulder with a smirk on her face. "You have to admit there are some services I don't provide that make up for the rest." She ducked when Hannah threw a pillow at her.

"I'm willing to settle for cooking these days. It's been so long since I've enjoyed any of the kind of 'services' you're talking about I've forgotten why I enjoyed them in the first place."

"Ask Santa. I hear he delivers for good girls. Although maybe that's just a rumor to make little Jewish girls jealous." Sarah was yelling from the kitchen by this time, well out of range of Hannah's pillow-throwing skills.

"Right. Santa bringing me a hot guy. With my luck I'd end up with one of his elves. Or a reindeer."

• • •

David Shay loved everything about the holiday season—the candles, the music, the decorations, even the crowds out on the rainy streets of Portland. He loved that he got to celebrate two winter holidays—he was Jewish and his family made a big deal out of Hanukkah. But his non-Jewish grandmother always made sure he enjoyed the Christmas season, too.

When he was a kid and people asked him what he wanted from Santa, David always said he was Jewish and Santa didn't come to his house. But before anyone could be embarrassed or feel sorry for him, he added, "Santa leaves my presents at Gramma's house," as if every Jewish kid had a non-Jewish relative who provided a place for Santa to leave his largesse.

As the head of the largest children's nonprofit program in Portland, David was happy to share his love for the season with the kids in the program. Usually it was a struggle to raise enough money so every one of the kids they served got something they needed, something they wanted, and something to read—the gift-giving mantra his grandmother had instilled in him. But not this year. The biggest independent bookstore in the city was donating books, and Simon Austin, owner of the only remaining locally owned retail operation, was underwriting the rest of the program.

Austin had promised David he and the employees of his eight women's stores would take care of the other two categories. Austin himself would make up the difference between what his employees collected and donated and what the program needed. In addition, there would be a generous cash donation by year's end to put the program's building campaign over the top. *And* Austin had volunteered to sponsor a holiday party for the program, at his expense and organized by the staff of his flagship store.

Simon Austin had visited the offices of SafePlace For Children and Parents the previous summer as part of a City Club of Portland committee studying the needs of children and young families in the city. David and Austin had hit it off immediately, and Austin's interest in David's program—which provided a range of services, from day care and medical help for low-income families to counseling and shelter for abused women and children—only grew with his work on the committee.

Thanks to Austin's interest, it was going to be a great holiday for SafePlace. That meant it would be a great holiday for David, who cared deeply about the program. Not just because it was his job to care, but also because the clients mattered to him. He poured his heart and soul into his work every day. Apparently that passion had convinced Simon Austin to care about SafePlace, too.

With two social workers as parents, it was unsurprising that David had ended up running a social services program. Growing up, he'd resisted the idea for a while—he couldn't see himself as an academic like his mother or a therapist like his father. But then he discovered an interest in nonprofit management. A degree in the subject and an internship with a program for victims of domestic abuse led him to SafePlace. After taking his first job there, he knew what he was meant to do with his life.

And now he was about to end a year of exciting growth and new opportunities with a bang. There would not only be enough money to make sure no kid was forgotten, but also a contribution for the building expansion, and a party to look forward to. What more could a guy want?

Well, maybe someone to share the season with. But even if David's grandmother hadn't been gone for the better part of a decade, he was pretty sure not even she could make that happen.

For more great novels from Peggy Bird, check out these titles:

A Holiday for Love series:

Praise for *Sparked by Love:*

"With lies and hidden agendas, you have to wait and see till the very end for all the pieces to fall together!"—Chicks That Read

"A warm, fuzzy romance read. Leo and Shannon are just so sweet together. There is plenty of steam as well. Very enjoyable read for romance lovers."—Wilovebooks, 4 stars

"This book had the Triple 'S' factor for me: short, sweet and sexy . . . a wonderful book."—Red's Hot Reads, 4 stars

"This was my first time reading Peggy Bird. I was pleasantly surprised by not only her writing style, which was very engaging and flowed, but also her characters."—Book Nerd, 4 stars

Praise for *Unmasking Love:*

"Spicy and modernized, this story relies on the mystique and romance of Romeo and Juliet, without the bad ending. Peggy Bird brings heat and heart to Halloween."—4 stars, I Am, Indeed

"I love the author's witty writing style, which is present right from the opening lines of this book. Ms. Bird successfully builds deliciously, believable sexual tension between Julie and Trace; you can almost hear the cracks of electricity!"—5 stars, Ellesea Loves Reading

"The story isn't long, but it wasn't rushed. ... Beautifully written and wonderfully engaging."—4 stars, Written Love Reviews

Second Chances series:

Praise for *Beginning Again*:

"Both Liz and Collins are great characters. Liz is not a bitter middle aged woman, but instead a very strong and brave lady. I really enjoyed *Beginning Again* because it was an easy read that made my gray autumn day a little bit less gray."—Long & Short Reviews

Praise for *Together Again*:

"…a very enjoyable romance. I loved the main characters and the great writing. I always admire strong, independent women, so if you also enjoy those qualities in a heroine, and enjoy a well-written romance, I recommend this one."—Night Owl Reviews

Praise for *Trusting Again*:

"The book moves along at a nice pace and the characters are believable and realistic. It is a well-written story with a wonderful ending!"—Harlequin Junkie

Loving Again
Believing Again
Falling Again

In the mood for more Crimson Romance?
Check out *A Man for All Seasons* by Mary Billiter at
CrimsonRomance.com.

9 781440 570421